I0566592

# MOONSHINER
# MYSTERY SOLVED

## SAM PEMBERTON

Copyright © 2024 Sam Pemberton
All cover art copyright © 2024 Sam Pemberton
All Rights Reserved

This is a fiction work. Names, places, characters and incidents are either the product of the author's imagination or are used fictitiously, and any resemblance to any actual persons, living or dead, businesses, organizations, events or locales is entirely coincidental.

No part of this book may be reproduced or transmitted in any form or by any means, electronic or mechanical, including photocopying, recording, or by any information storage and retrieval system, without permission in writing from the author.

Publishing Coordinator – Sharon Kizziah-Holmes

Paperback-Press
an imprint of A & S Publishing
Paperback Press, LLC
Springfield, Missouri

ISBN - 978-1-964559-18-6

# DEDICATION

*Moonshiner Mystery Solved* is the final book in the Moonshiner series. It is dedicated to the memory of Nancy Dailey for the work she did in the beginning. She set the tone for all the books and her work on *Missy's Life as a Slave* was the last one, she was able to do

# ACKNOWLEDGMENTS

Lael Kennedy has done a great job picking up from where Nancy left off in her editing. Thank you for your hard work, young lady. I appreciate all you've done.

I can never say enough about Sharon Kizziah-Holmes and the work she does as the publishing coordinator.

Also, I would be remiss if I didn't talk about my wife, Patricia Pemberton, she not only is the proofreader, but she is the glue that brings everything together.

These ladies are the best and have made it possible for the books to be published.

# CHAPTER 1

The sycamore tree at the end of the swinging bridge was casting a shadow that reached far into the field below the bridge. Shadows from the bridge accented the sycamore tree. The cables supporting the bridge appeared to be upside down arches as they extended the width of the field. Early morning shadows shortened as the sun continued to rise when Willie Sitton arrived at the barn.

Sweltering heat was unusual this early in the morning. There was no breeze. Even before the sun came up, the pre-dawn mist was uncomfortable.

The bridge on Big Creek was the gathering place for people to swim and get away from the heat. They had not started arriving yet. It was still early in the day. Willie left the barn and went to the blacksmith shop.

His thoughts were interrupted by the sound of a truck loaded with logs crossing the bridge. Sounds from the engine were louder than the creaking of the boards. Heavy trucks always stretched the cables supporting the bridge tight, but they were silent. The wall of the barn echoed the sounds of the engine and the creaking of the boards. All of these sounds grew louder because of the continuous pull over the planks of the bridge as they sagged. Willie liked to watch a log truck crossing the bridge and was amazed the old bridge was still holding up after all the years.

The sound of the log truck changed when it came off the bridge. Willie did not recognize the driver or the truck as it passed the blacksmith shop. The flat gravel road was an easier pull than crossing the bridge. He watched as the log truck went out of sight, up the hill from the creek.

The road was now 14 Highway. Willie didn't remember who oversaw the maintenance when the bridge was built. Now workers came from the Arkansas Highway Department at least once a month to check the boards in the bridge floor and to re-nail any loose ones.

Willie didn't hear or see Preacher Ed as he drove across the bridge. He was inspecting the tools waiting to be sharpened and checking the board to see if any of them were due to be picked up. There were two hoes tied together, and according to the color of the tie, they belonged to Jess Still's grandson. They were late.

It was too hot to fire up the forge. Willie put the tools back in the bin as he heard Preacher Ed slam his car door. Preacher Ed stepped away from the car and paused as he looked back. Willie thought he was checking the tires because getting tubes and tires for cars had become a problem during the war. Preacher Ed walked away from the car without greeting Willie.

Willie observed Preacher Ed. His mind went back over the last twenty years to when they first met at Hickory Hollow. The tall, slim young man was now a graying older gentleman. He was still tall; his shoulders were not slumped. He was still about the same weight, and he stood straight. Even in the hot weather he was wearing his usual vest over a long-sleeve shirt with the cuffs buttoned.

Willie smiled when he thought of the flask inside the

vest on his left side. Preacher Ed no longer picked up his moonshine from the stump where Willie had left quarts of moonshine for Coy Bryant; he got it from Willie at the barn. Willie wasn't sure how much the little flask contained that the preacher carried in his vest pocket, nor did he know how often he refilled it. He didn't keep track of how much moonshine Preacher Ed got. He gave it to him.

Maybe he gave it to him because of guilt carried over from years ago when Willie got the preacher to start drinking. Drinking had not affected preacher's voice; it was as strong as the first day Willie heard him at Hickory Hollow. The only change in the preacher's appearance was his face showed signs of worry from losing a baby shortly after birth and then having his son Noah die in a training accident at Fort Dix, New Jersey.

Even if the years had not been kind to the preacher, Willie Sitton was still his best friend. Standing alongside each other, they were an unusual pair. Willie at, five-foot-eight, tried to avoid standing next to Preacher Ed, who was over six feet tall. Willie's paunchy stomach made him look even shorter. Willie's hair was an off-color gray. In his younger days, his hair was a dark brown, but as he got older it tended to drift toward a grayish blonde. The color of his hair bothered Willie, but he still didn't wear a hat.

Preacher Ed always wore a hat. It was always set perched on the top of his head sitting well above his ears, but Willie never told him that the hat didn't look right. Their friendship dealt with personal convictions and opinions about other people's lives. They never discussed their personal appearance.

Preacher Ed still came to the barn often. Usually, he stopped to visit when he was on his way to Marshall. Most of his trips to Marshall were to visit patients in the new hospital. His car was a four-door roadster that didn't need to be cranked. Willie still refused to buy an automobile. He never intended to drive, although, he enjoyed riding with

Preacher Ed.

Preacher Ed walked past Willie toward the barn. He still had not greeted Willie. Willie followed him inside the barn where the poker games were always held. Preacher Ed sat down immediately. Willie was standing across from him. The big cut of wood used as a poker table was between them.

"I brought a letter I want you to read him,'' Preacher Ed said as he tossed the letter onto the poker table. The big cut of wood was used to cards being tossed onto it; money was always exchanged on top of it, and mortgages had been written and signed to cover gambling debts. This was the first time a letter was ever tossed onto it.

"That's a letter Alan Bryant wrote to Jim Rhodes."

"You want me to read it?" Willie asked.

"Jim said for me to bring it to you," was the preacher's answer.

Willie picked up the envelope and took out the letter.

# CHAPTER 2

W illie put the letter back into the envelope after he finished reading it. He tossed it back onto the poker table where it had been when he picked it up.

"What is Alan trying to say?" he asked Preacher Ed.

"I don't know," Preacher Ed answered.

"When I read it, it sounded like he thought we know more than we do."

"Do you think he's talking about what happened when Coy and Ruth got shot?"

*"I'm not doing very well, Jim. I would really like to visit with Cousin Willie and Preacher Ed,"* Willie quoted. He picked up the envelope and began reading the letter again.

*I believe they can clear up a lot of questions I've had in my mind for years,* Alan had continued to write.

*If you could, have Willie bring that boy of his, Carl Harris, and bring Haskell's son-in-law, the Tabor boy.* Willie wondered why Alan would want to visit with the four of them.

Preacher Ed stood silently. Willie walked around the poker table and looked at the letter he had placed back on the table without putting it back into the envelope.

"Jim gave you that letter?" he asked Preacher Ed.

Before the preacher could answer, Willie began reviewing the circumstances of the letter.

"He has to be talking about when the shooting happened," Willie added curiously, not quite as a question.

Preacher Ed remained silent. Then he began to explain his thoughts.

"You are family. Alan wrote this to Jim, they are cousins. Jim asked me to bring it to you, another cousin. But why does he want me to come with you to visit? I'm not kin to any of you."

Preacher Ed stopped for a minute. He walked the same circle around the poker table as Willie had walked earlier, stopping for a moment and taking a drink from the flask he carried in his vest. It was barely a sip. Willie watched as he put the lid back on and stuck it back inside his vest. He always carried it with the curved portion toward his body. Willie was still wondering how much actual liquor the little flask held.

The letter had been lying on the stool for over an hour. Willie had asked a few questions, including one that still went unanswered.

"Have you seen Alan lately? Do you think there's something wrong with him? We are just guessing that he wants to talk about the shooting," he would say on almost every trip he made around the room.

Preacher Ed laughed. "Why are we walking in circles in this room and guessing about something when all we have got to do is make a trip to Alan's place and find out what's going on?" It was more a statement than a question.

Willie kept the letter, placing it back in the envelope, and followed the preacher as he returned to his automobile. They would decide what to do later.

The creek was getting low. The water was still cold but was warming up every day as the weather continued to get warmer. June of 1944 brought a lot of change to the area. Over the last twenty years, the number of automobiles had increased a lot. Willie was standing on the rock where he had caught fish ever since he was a boy. He remembered catching a smallmouth bass while he was fishing with a cane pole. The bass was too large for the pole to hold up, and he had trapped it on the rock to keep from losing it.

He had come to the creek early this morning after he fed the hogs. He found out that if he got there early before anyone came to swim, he could kill a couple of bass with a gig he had made. The gig was a cross between a pitch gig and the gig that was used to kill fish underneath rocks. He made several of the long-pronged narrow gigs for people to kill catfish under rocks in White River and Buffalo River. They had taken out some large yellow catfish by killing them with the long-pronged gigs. He stood still, watching the space between the two rocks where he had always stood when he tried to kill one of the bass as it traveled between the rocks.

A lot of things have changed. He thought it was illegal for him to kill a "game fish"—the name they had given to all the fish that would bite a live bait. He wondered about all the changes in laws. During the Depression, a lot of money was spent building roads and bridges. The 1940s had seen the start of World War II. The draft had taken most of the young men to the Army. Carl Harris, Pauline's husband, was turned down on his physical. It bothered Willie that Carl had an enlarged heart, and he wasn't sure he'd ever heard of one before, but he was proud that Carl had got to stay home and was helping him.

They were only making about four runs of moonshine a year. The government was everywhere—they were building roads; they were drafting the young men. There were laws controlling almost everything. Willie had even filed an income tax. The banker told him if he didn't, and they checked his account, they would take his money. Willie didn't know whether he was happy with all the changes or not.

The last few days he had read and reread the letter Alan Bryant wrote to Jim Rhodes. Preacher Ed came by and suggested they try to go see Alan on Thursday of the week before the Fourth of July.

Willie stopped thinking about the letter. He gouged the gig through the largest smallmouth bass he had seen in years. He carried the fish across the creek, leaving it on the gig while he cleaned it and got it ready to take to the house. There was going to be some fish fried very shortly for lunch at the Sitton house.

# CHAPTER 3

Judging by where the sun was hitting the porch, it was almost noon. Willie could smell the fish frying. Ellen was preparing lunch. Willie had heard that term the last time he was in Marshall. The Sitton clan always ate breakfast, dinner, and then supper. Willie laughed to himself when he tried to recall all the changes. He was born in 1878. The earliest memories he had were stories about settling on Big Creek, then continuing all the way up through the Civil War.

Now, there had been at least a dozen automobiles that passed after he brought the fish to the house. Carl and Pauline bought a car. It was a used roadster with a rumble seat. The worst ride Willie and Ellen ever took in his life was when Pauline convinced them to ride to Rock Creek Cemetery in the rumble seat.

Willie had spent most of the time since Preacher Ed brought the letter trying to figure out why Alan wanted him and Preacher Ed to bring Carl and Seth to see him. He was sure It had to be something to do with the shooting. Carl and Seth were witnesses to the rider and horse leaving the barn.

*Was it Alan who did the shooting?* Willie wondered. *Me and Preacher Ed figured out it was impossible for him to be there at the right time.*

"Come on, let's eat!" Ellen called out to Willie.

Willie took a drink of the glass of tea. The tea had ice in it. There was an ice box on the porch for the delivery of big chunks of ice. It was something else that started during the Depression years. A salesman came by, offering to leave one of the boxes if they would buy ice twice a week. They agreed to it. It was one of the advantages of having the roads and the automobiles. The icehouse was located about halfway between Marshall and Leslie, by the railroad track. Willie didn't know if they were able to freeze ice or if it came in by train. Either way, there was ice on the porch, and there was a space for keeping the butter and other things that used to stay in the spring box.

When he ate the fish, Willie took the large tailpiece and noticed how the tail fin was fried to perfection. It was his favorite piece to eat. Carl and Willie reached a truce on dividing the fish when they ate together. They split the crispy, fried tail fins. For the first five years after Carl arrived at the bridge, they all ate together, even after Pauline and Carl were married. When the granddaughters were born, Pauline started cooking at home.

"Jim came by yesterday while you and Carl were up the creek repairing the Watergate," Ellen said as she passed the latest version of Johnny cakes to Willie. Willie didn't answer but picked up a couple of Johnny cakes, a combination of cornmeal and flour with bits of onion added to them. Pauline had fried the Johnny cakes in the same grease after she finished frying the fish. Carl took a bite.

"These things are really good," Willie said. He still hadn't answered the comment about Jim Rhodes coming by to see Ellen. After all, it wasn't uncommon for his wife's brother to stop and visit.

"Did you hear what I said about Jim coming by?" Ellen asked.

"Yeah, I heard you," Willie finally answered, taking another bite of fish and eating a green onion with the Johnny cake. He finished chewing before he added, "What did he have to say?"

"He said he gave a letter from Alan Bryant to Preacher Ed and that Preacher Ed had left it with you after you read it."

Ellen's comment surprised Willie. He didn't realize that Preacher Ed would tell Jim that he left the letter with him.

"We could not make heads or tails of what that letter meant" Willie said.

"It's about the shooting. Alan is worried after all these years about who-knows-what," Ellen said.

"I don't know what you mean," Willie answered. "The sheriff accused Jim of doing the shooting, but he proved he was in Sylamore."

After several minutes of discussion of all the people that had been questioned about the shooting, Willie and Ellen both agreed they didn't see any reason to rehash all of it twenty years later.

Willie left to go back to the barn and hoped Preacher Ed would come by before the afternoon was over.

# CHAPTER 4

Willie decided to go ahead and fire up the forge in the blacksmith shop. He would get the two hoes sharpened for the Still's boy. His mind went back to the time when Jess Still fell off the bluff while hunting. Everybody blamed Willie because Jess was drinking the moonshine he bought from Willie. Willie stopped selling for a time after the accident. Jess's son was the owner of the hoes. He was just a baby when his dad died in the coon hunting accident. Willie started cranking the bellows to heat up the coal in the forge while his mind wandered back in time.

He began reviewing all the things said after the shooting in Coy Bryant's barn. When Preacher Ed brought the letter, that was the first time there'd been any discussions about the shooting for a good number of years. During the time he was eating the fish with Ellen, his mind started racing back through everything that happened immediately after the shooting.

He remembered Seth Tabor was questioned by Sheriff

Joe Carson because he watched from the bluff above the barn.

Joe Carson told Willie, "That Tabor boy got a better look at the horse and rider than Carl did because he didn't have to control a team of mules."

Willie went over all the theories with him, that he and Preacher Ed came up with after the shooting. They decided it was impossible to accuse Alan Bryant of shooting his brother. After reading the letter several times, Willie wasn't sure why Alan would want Carl and Seth to come to see him.

The letter had to be about the shooting. There was no other reason Willie could think of, that Alan would want to see the only two witnesses to the horse leaving the barn.

The first hoe was hotter than Willie needed it to start hammering a new point. A smile came to his face while he was letting the hoe cool a little bit before striking it with a hammer. The anvil drew the heat out and he started beating the new point on to the hoe.

Carl was standing behind him before Willie knew he was there. Willie had not mentioned the letter Preacher Ed brought to Carl.

"What are you doing sneaking up behind me?" Willie asked.

"I didn't want to disturb you," Carl answered.

Willie finished pounding the hammer on the anvil and began grinding the finish point on the hoe.

"I've been needing you to come by today," Willie said to Carl.

"Why?" Carl asked.

"I want you to read a letter Alan Bryant wrote Jim Rhodes. Preacher Ed brought it to me."

# CHAPTER 5

W illie gave the envelope with the letter in it to Carl. Carl sat down on one of the stools and unfolded the letter on the card table, the large cut of wood used for the card games.

"Willie, open the door, I need some light to see this," Carl said.

Willie watched Carl's emotions as he read the letter. He didn't see any expressions until Carl read the line where Alan had written. *"If you could, have Willie bring that boy of his, Carl Harris..."*

Carl immediately backed up and read the letter again. This time, after reading a few lines, he would stop and look away for a minute.

"Have you got any idea why Alan would want to see all four of us together?" Carl asked Willie.

"No more than you do." Willie's voice was sharp and had an edge to it.

Carl handed the envelope and letter back to Willie.

Willie continued to watch Carl, waiting for his next

reaction. He studied Carl's face much in the same way he would poker players sitting with him at the table, but the cards on the table were never as interesting as the letter from Alan to Jim Rhodes. In poker, a winner was easily determined, and the money divided, but this letter presented questions not easily answered.

Carl was glad when all the questions ended years ago. Pauline and Carl had been able to visit with Seth and Melissa whenever they saw them at any kind of social function. Since they got the car, they had been able to go to decorate at the Rock Creek Cemetery, where Noah Sitton was buried many years ago, long before Carl left the burning house west of Big Creek. During all these times spent in the presence of each other, neither Carl nor Seth ever mentioned the day at the barn.

After reading the letter, Carl wondered if Seth ever recognized Alan Bryant's horse. He tried to forget about the day he saw the horse as it left the courthouse in Marshall. He rode home without any conversation with Willie after he saw it. He remembered all the discussions about how impossible it would be for Alan to know when to hide in the loft of the barn and shoot Coy and Sister Rhodes.

Those questions irritated Carl, and he didn't see why they needed to be answered now. After seeing the letter, Carl knew there was still not anything that could be explained or answered. There were no plans to go see Alan. Carl wondered if they would bump into Seth and Melissa at Big Flat. Pauline expected them to go to Jim Rhodes's mercantile in Big Flat on Saturdays, or to go to Marshall so she could shop in the stores around the town square.

It was much easier to go to Big Flat. After crossing the bridge, the road went up by Cedar Grove schoolhouse and then stayed on a level plane while winding around the heads of the hollows until it came out in bare branch. It then followed the hollow until it climbed the hill at the head of "bare branch". After the hill, it was only a short distance before the road stayed on a level plane the rest of the way to Jim Rhodes's store. It was an easier buggy trip years ago, and now it was a much easier trip in a car than following the winding road to Marshall.

Highway 14 went north to Yellville at Hickory Hollow, and the recently-named Highway 27 went by everybody's house on its way to Marshall and eventually wound along Brushy Creek before going directly up a hollow to the town square. The last trip Carl and Pauline made; he fixed four flats. Carl never told Willie when he asked why they didn't get home until after dark.

While Willie was ready to go with someone in their car, he still was too stubborn to admit it was an improvement over his horse and buggy. Carl's thoughts continued to ramble after he read the letter and started home.

*"Why?"* continued to be the dominant thought.

"Was Alan Bryant older than Willie?" Carl asked himself. He knew Willie was well into his seventies, and Preacher Ed was a few years younger. What Carl was trying to ask was, "What would three old men be asking when they got to Alan's Bryant's house for the visit?''

He stopped reviewing the letter and questioning himself when he got home.

"Mama said that Daddy's got a letter Preacher Ed brought to him from Alan Bryant, Mama's cousin and Jim Rhodes's cousin. It was written to Jim, but he wanted Preacher Ed to bring it to Dad." Pauline stopped to think after the rambling description of the letter. She then asked, "Have you read it?''

Carl's face flushed. He tried to decipher Pauline's description of the letter. After thinking for a minute, he answered.

"Yes, I've read it." He continued in a tone that told Pauline he didn't like the question. "I don't know what to make of it, and I don't know for sure if I will go with them."

He went through the house to the back porch and dipped water from the bucket into the washbasin. He washed his hands and face. The cold water felt good. It was a hot June afternoon. The discussions of things from the distant past had just added to the heat of the day.

# CHAPTER 6

Sunday afternoons were time for swimming and picnics at the bridge below Willie's barn. Sometimes a group of people would interrupt the swimming to have baptismal services. The people swimming were expected to get out of the way and not interfere with the church service. It was considered absolute blasphemy for a swimmer to dive off the rock beside where the baptism was being held.

Carl and Pauline had two girls old enough to swim. Pauline bought bathing suits without asking Carl. He found out later that all the children who attended Cedar Grove school had bathing suits. He liked to go to the swimming hole. You never knew who was going to show up to swim. This afternoon Seth and Melissa Tabor came.

"Carl, how are you doing?" Seth asked as he sat down on the gravel a few feet away from Carl.

Carl had been laying back with an elbow supporting his head. He sat up. He drew his knees up under his chin and leaned forward looking toward the water before he answered Seth.

"I've been doing fine, just trying to survive the hot weather," he finally answered.

"Preacher Ed came to see me and told me about the letter he left with Willie," Seth said.

Carl relaxed, extending his left arm out and turning to face Seth before he said anything.

"I read the letter," Carl said. "As a matter of fact, I read it several times."

"What do you think Alan wants?" Seth asked. Before Carl could answer he continued. "Haskell went to see him last week. " Seth was referring to Melissa's dad. "He said Alan is really not doing well at all."

Seth stood up and looked around. He was trying to figure out where Melissa was sitting before he continued. "He's got something wrong with his breathing, and he's lost a lot of weight."

Carl still hadn't made a comment. He understood that Seth's father-in-law was a brother to Alan Bryant and Coy. Haskell Bryant would have firsthand information. But the condition of his health still didn't answer the question of why he wanted to see Preacher Ed, Willie, Carl and Seth.

"The only possible reason he would have for wanting me and you there, Carl, is he knows we saw the rider and the horse leaving the barn after Coy was shot." Seth sat down on the gravel about an arm-length from Carl.

They sat silently. They watched the children trying to learn to swim by scooting off one rock and pushing toward another. An older boy that neither Seth nor Carl recognized was serving as their teacher. If one of the children had trouble making it to the rock, he would help them. The kids were having fun. During the time Carl sat trying to decide what he wanted to say, one of the children suddenly became able to swim and swam a circle before coming back to the rock. Several of the kids applauded and were proud he was able to swim.

"Are you going to go, Seth?" Carl asked about the trip to see Alan.

"I'll have to go. Haskell and Melissa expect me to," Seth answered with no enthusiasm.

"I'll go with you," Carl added. "Let's ride together, and that way we won't have to answer Preacher Ed and Willie's questions if we don't ride with them."

Once again, they remained silent. Each one of them wondered what the other one was thinking. Seth knew the horse he saw in Alan's corral was the same horse he saw climbing the hill after the shooting. He didn't say a word to Carl. Carl wondered if Seth knew that the horse, which he saw at Marshall was the horse leaving the barn after the shooting.

They didn't have any further discussion. Pauline walked up and said, "I've invited Melissa and Seth to the house for supper."

They left the creek and went to Carl and Pauline's. The cabin where Carl was living had been expanded several times to accommodate their family.

Seth had never been there before, and it took several minutes for Carl to explain all the different times the house was remodeled. They eventually finished the tour and sat in the rocker's, facing Big Creek while listening to the children playing in the yard.

It had been a fun Sunday afternoon, but the questions about the trip to see Alan Bryant were still in the back of their minds.

# CHAPTER 7

M onday was even hotter than the week before. Carl went to the barn, as usual, and didn't see Willie anywhere. He hitched the mules to the wagon and loaded four salt blocks to take up the creek and put them in different pastures. It was getting drier, and the creek was getting lower.

While the kids were swimming on Sunday, they didn't come out of the water shivering and complaining about the water being cold. Carl stood on the back of the wagon and looked at the creek where the Hickory branch ran in. It was one of the bigger holes of water along this stretch of the creek. There were a couple of smallmouth bass staying still in the water just above the shoal. He watched them closely. He was always amazed how they could hold their position without seeming to move at all. Occasionally there was a noticeable movement in their dorsal fins, or maybe just a slight flick of their tail fin. He watched until they gave a sudden surge to the top and swallowcd a minnow that hc only noticed just an instant before they swallowed it. They were watching the top water minnows and laying out at exactly the right depth to come to the surface and swallow them.

The mules took a drink from the creek as the wagon crossed before heading into the field where the cows and calves were being kept. It was not midmorning, but the cows had finished grazing and were already laying in the shade of the trees along the creek bank. Hot weather changed their habits. None of the calves were laying down. Some of the calves were grazing on the grass along the creek bank and eating leaves from the tree limbs they could reach.

Carl placed one of the salt blocks in the trough where he usually put grain for the cattle. There was still enough grass that the cattle were not being fed at this time. He left that field and went on up the creek to check on the steers. Not much thought was being given to the letter Preacher Ed brought to the barn.

Carl returned to the barn around noon. The sound of Willie hitting the anvil could be heard a long distance before the mules pulled into the barn lot. After unharnessing the mules, he turned them into the barn lot. They had access to the creek for water. He did not rub them down or give them any special attention. During the day, he had not noticed any problems with their shoes or harness. The team was in good shape for the time of the year. He dumped over a gallon of grain mixed with salt into their trough. The mules needed extra salt to work in hot weather.

Willie had stopped hammering in the shop.

"It's too hot for this," Willie said as Carl walked into the shop.

"What are you sharpening today?" Carl asked.

"When that Still boy picked up his hoes, he left these two Mattocks to be sharpened," Willie answered. A Mattock hoe had a huge blade on one side with a sharp pick on the other side.

"He uses them to cut sprouts out of his pastures. He says if you cut sprouts in hot weather they will never come back," Willie explained.

There were six goats on the Sitton farm. Willie moved them to the fields after the grass got too short for the cows to graze. Carl always wondered why the goats stayed where Willie wanted them. He had always heard goats were a nuisance, wouldn't stay anywhere and would eat anything. But for Willie, they kept the sprouts down. Carl was glad. He had cut sprouts once. If you missed with the hoe, the sprout could recoil and whack you in the side of the head. Cutting sprouts was not something he enjoyed doing and hoped he never had to do it again.

"Ellen said. Seth and Melissa visited you and Pauline yesterday," Willie said as he started toward the barn.

Following about ten feet behind, Carl didn't answer until they were inside the barn.

"Yeah, they visited with their kids. It was a good visit." Carl did not add any details.

"You and Seth going with me and the preacher to see Alan?'' Willie asked.

"Yeah, we're going, but we're gonna ride by ourselves" he answered Willie.

"Why do you want to do that?" Willie sounded irritated.

"We want to visit and get better acquainted," Carl gave as an excuse.

He did not want to tell Willie that neither he nor Seth wanted to spend a long time in an automobile with Preacher Ed and him. They were sure it would be a continual flow of questions about why Alan wanted to see them. And they did not want to discuss what they saw at the barn unless it was necessary.

"Fred Hudson told the preacher last Sunday at Cozy that if we were going to see Alan, we needed to go," Willie said as he sat down in the corner away from the poker table.

"Reckon what's going on with Alan?" Carl asked.

"I don't know." Willie stood back up and walked closer to Carl.

Willie opened the crib door and took out a quart of the good moonshine. He kept it for very special occasions. Carl wondered what he was about to do. It was too hot to drink today. Willie took two cups that were hanging on the wall and poured a small amount in each one.

"This whiskey is for sipping and thinking." he said with a laugh. "We've got to think about this trip to see Alan."

Willie began a long monologue about why Alan would want to see them. He talked about the fact there had been no discussions in several years about who did the shooting at Coy Bryant's barn. The combination of a preacher, a moonshiner, and the two people who witnessed the rider leaving the barn, could only mean one thing. Alan Bryant had something he wanted to get off his chest before he passed away.

"We have no way of knowing why Alan is wanting us there," Willie finally said. "We will just have to go and listen to what he has to say."

Willie stood back up before adding, "I don't know anything firsthand, except the preacher caught them in the glade and then over a year later they got shot in the barn doing what they were doing in the glade."

Carl was irritated with the whole idea of being questioned again about the shooting.

# CHAPTER 8

The graves in Rock Creek Cemetery were cleaned off in July every year. Cleaning the graves and removing dead flowers was usually planned for just after the fourth. A lot of people who lived away would come back twice a year. There was always a decoration early in the year, and the old flowers were trimmed and removed after the heat of summer began.

Carl and Pauline were at the annual Fourth of July picnic at the Cedar Grove schoolhouse, but they hadn't seen Seth or Melissa.

Carl was looking at Noah Sitton's tomb when Seth walked up behind him.

"How are you doing, Carl?" Seth asked.

"Doing good," Carl turned to face him.

"Are you gonna be ready to make the trip to Melissa's uncle's house this next week?" Seth asked.

Carl wasn't sure how to answer. He walked away in a circle trying to think of what to say. When Carl returned, Seth continued.

"I passed by where Willie was visiting with Preacher Ed and Fred Hudson. They're planning on going Thursday." Seth pointed to the tree by the gate to the cemetery. They were all three still standing there, visiting.

"Is Fred Hudson going too?" Carl asked.

"I think that's what I overheard," Seth said. "They pointed at you and asked if we were going." Before Carl could say anything, Seth added," I didn't say anything, I just walked up here to talk to you.

"I wonder if Alan is going to question us or just tell us something," Carl said.

"We will just have to go and find out," Seth answered.

The plans were made. Carl and Seth went to the tree where Willie and Preacher Ed were visiting with Fred Hudson. They agreed to leave early on Thursday to go see Alan.

Fred Hudson and Seth were going to meet them at the Hickory Hollow junction of Highway 14 and 27. They were going to go through Marshall and take Highway 65 up to St. Joe before going east to Alan's farm.

There was no discussion of who Fred Hudson would ride with. Carl just hoped Fred would ride with Willie and Preacher Ed. He got an uneasy feeling about what he knew and wondered if Seth might know the horse at the barn was Alan's.

He was not going to admit to it, even if he and Seth got into a discussion about the shooting. He had grown so tired of all the questions years ago just after the murders. Until Preacher Ed brought the letter Alan wrote to Jim Rhodes, there had not been any discussions or questions for the last several years. Now, they were making a trip to see Alan Bryant on his deathbed.

Carl watched the sunset as the shadows crept up the hill behind the house. It was peaceful. A cool breeze was coming from the east down the hollow. The darker it got, the cooler the breeze got. The silence of dusk began to give way to the sound of the night. An owl flew into the gum tree and landed near the top. It was the tallest tree in the hollow. The sounds of its wings fluttering as it landed were barely audible but the screech it gave echoed across the hollow. Its sound barely faded before another owl answered somewhere up the Hickory Hollow.

It was soothing to listen to the sounds of the night. Pauline was getting the girls ready for bed. She came out and joined Carl. They sat quietly, listening as more sounds followed the owls screeching. A fox added its voice to the sounds of the night. Carl could envision the fox catching a rabbit for its evening meal. Pauline broke the silence.

"You're going with Daddy to see Alan?" she asked.

Carl just nodded. She placed her hand on his shoulder and did not comment for a few minutes.

"I guess you're wondering what all of this is about?" she finally said. "Me and Mama were guessing years ago about who could have done the shooting. We never could come up with anybody."

Carl still hadn't joined her in conversation.

"That happened the first year you got here, didn't it?" Pauline continued. "That's been over twenty years now."

Carl looked away, trying to imagine Pauline in conversations about what he saw at the barn. She had never tried to discuss it with him until now. A couple of questions ran through his mind. He wondered how many other women had discussed the shooting, and who they guessed the shooter was. "Mama said they first accused Uncle Jim of being the shooter, but he proved he was in Sylamore." Pauline was determined to keep the discussion going even if Carl was not going to join in. "Aunt Ruth was a bad woman. Mama said Uncle Jim should never have married her."

"That's the first time I've ever thought of her as being your aunt." Carl finally joined the conversation.

After he said that, a memory of Sister Rhodes laying in

the loft of the barn came to mind—a visual of a body with its chin on its chest and the eyes staring at the naked boobs.

"How old were we when that happened?'' Pauline said. Before he could answer, she replied to herself. "I had just turned thirteen, and you were fifteen. It was three years before we got married."

This whole conversation and everything that had been discussed since Preacher Ed brought the letter to the barn was irritating to Carl. Something which happened over twenty years ago needed to be left in the past. He hoped when he met Seth and they went to see Alan, that would be the end of it.

# CHAPTER 9

It was just breaking dawn when Carl got to the barn. Thursday was the day of the trip to see Alan. He walked past the barn out onto the bridge. Willie told him to get there as early as possible because Preacher Ed would be there shortly after daylight. Carl was almost in the middle of the bridge before he noticed Willie standing next to the guardrail facing up the creek. The swimming hole was shining through the darkness as the sun was just starting to come up. One of Wille's favorite things was watching daybreak.

"You ready to go this morning, Carl?" Wille's voice lacked enthusiasm.

Carl leaned over the bridge and looked down before he answered. "Yeah, I guess," his tone matched Willie's.

They heard a vehicle coming down the hill from the west, headed toward Big Flat. It was a log truck. It was traveling much faster than most cars and trucks on the gravel road. Neither Willie nor Carl had time to get off the bridge. The truck came onto the bridge and didn't have any headlights. Willie and Carl turned facing the center of the bridge and stood as close as possible to the guardrail as the truck went by.

"Did they ever see us?" Willie asked as the truck passed and left the bridge heading up the road toward the Cedar Creek schoolhouse.

"No, I don't know if they did or not," Carl answered. "Who was that? I didn't recognize the truck or the driver."

"I don't know either, there were three of them in the cab," Willie answered. They stood, listening as the truck went out of hearing to the east. There was still no sign of Preacher Ed coming to the bridge.

"Are you taking your car? "Willie directed the question to Carl.

"No, I was going to ride with you and Preacher Ed to Hickory and then with Seth in his pickup truck," Carl said.

The sun was getting hot by the time Preacher Ed, Willie and Carl arrived at the junction of Highways 14 and 27. The Hickory Hollow store was open, and people were fixing flats and pumping gas.

"People with cars and trucks never do anything but pump gas and fix flats, "Willie muttered.

Seth and Fred Hudson arrived a few minutes after Preacher Ed parked the car.

"How are we riding?" Preacher Ed asked.

Carl spoke up. "Me and Seth are going to follow you."

They were following the preacher's car and trying to stay far enough back to not be in his dust. They started out close, and when they passed a car, they almost had a collision because they could not see it through the dust. Seth laughed and told Carl, "We are going to stay back far enough to let the dust clear, that was almost one of them wrecks."

They didn't make it over a few miles until Preacher Ed pulled off the road underneath the shade of a tree.

"We got a problem. I'm losing air in the right front tire;

we might as well fix it here in the shade."

The frown on Willie's face spoke louder than the preacher's words.

Seth and Carl removed the tire and patched the tube. They put it back on the rim and began pumping it full of air.

"How many flats do you think we will have today?" Seth directed the question to Carl.

"Me and Pauline had four on our last trip to Marshall and back," Carl answered.

Flats had become an absolute nuisance since the start of the war. The production of tires and tubes had been diverted to the war effort, and personal automobiles were on the ration list. Preacher Ed was waiting for replacements, and it had been over six months since he received a coupon entitling him to them. Still no new tires and tubes.

"It's a good thing they are not rationing the patches, or I would've had to have parked this car months ago," Preacher Ed entered the conversation.

Neither Carl nor Seth told him they had to remove three old patches and replace them, which was the reason for the flat.

The interruption to fix the flat ended. It had been almost an hour, and they were on the pavement of Highway 65 heading north to St. Joe. There was no more dust. There was no more trouble with having flats. Seth was having difficulty keeping up with the preacher.

"Preacher Ed's next problem is not going to be a flat, he's going to flip over," Seth said, worried. "Thirty-five miles per hour is too fast around these curves."

Neither him nor Carl had ever considered the old men could be a problem to keep up with.

They stopped across from the depot in St. Joe at the Mercantile. The store was bigger than Jim Rhodes's store in Big Flat. They were able to get a cold bottle of Coca-

Cola from the icebox with the Coca-Cola sign. There were several of those types of ice boxes scattered around at various merchants. Jim Rhodes needed to get one for the store in Big Flat.

"I'm going to tell Jim he's going to start losing business if he doesn't get one of the Coca-Cola boxes." Preacher Ed said as they finished drinking their Cokes.

It took a while to get directions on how to get to Alan Bryant's farm. While every one of them had been there, it was their first trip by automobile and following the county roads. The manager of the mercantile told them there were three low-water bridges, but "As dry it is there won't be a problem crossing the creeks."

Carl was getting nervous. He wondered what the meeting was going to be like once they got to Alan Bryant's. There had been no discussion about the meeting between him and Seth. They talked about their children, talked about their wives, and they commented on all the farms they passed along with the cars they met.

They were consciously avoiding any discussion of the purpose of the trip.

# CHAPTER 10

When they left St. Joe, heading east, it was still before noon. The road was straight. It was following along beside the railroad track, just a few feet away from the rails. At times, it would swing away from the train track to create room for a crossing. The rails of the train tracks were several feet above the roadbed for cars. It was a smooth gravel road. Preacher Ed was driving much slower than he did earlier in the day before the flat. The time they had lost while they fixed the tire was made up by how fast he had driven on Highway 65.

The road suddenly turned to the north and went down a hill leaving the railroad tracks behind. There was one steep hill with a curve, and then it straightened out, running just south of a dry creek bed. There was a gravel crossing that took them slightly to the north. The road turned at a sharp curve and went down a steep embankment and Seth and Carl watched as Preacher Ed hit the water on the low-water bridge faster than he intended to.

"He will drown his engine out hittin' the water that

fast," Seth commented.

They watched as Preacher Ed's car sputtered a couple of times and then smoothed out and went on.

"He got lucky, the engine was hot enough to dry out and keep running," Seth commented again.

Carl had not contributed anything to the conversation. Noticing the farmsteads since they left St. Joe had kept Carl busy. There were several nice homes built on each side of the road. It appeared some of the merchants in St. Joe had farms within a couple of miles of their business. Carl wasn't sure anyone could make enough money farming to build the houses they were passing.

"You think these houses we've been passing before we got to the water crossing belonged to farmers?'' he asked Seth.

"I don't know," Seth replied. "There is a lot more money around Leslie and Marshall and St. Joe, more than there is on the ridges along Big Creek. Willie Sitton and Haskell Bryant, our fathers-in-law have got as much money as anybody, they just want to keep living like pioneers. I can't imagine either one of them spending the money to build one of these houses we have passed."

Carl didn't answer. He was overwhelmed in his thoughts. He had never considered anything better than what he and Pauline had on Big Creek. Ever since he got to the bridge, his only goal had been to survive. Maybe he had become like Willie. He never said it, but he wondered if Seth had done the same thing. He knew from the things Melissa told Pauline that Haskell felt the same way about automobiles as Willie. They were riding in a pickup truck because Seth and Melissa convinced Haskell it was practical to have a pickup because they could haul things for the farm.

"What are you going to do when we get to the Alan Bryant's house?'' Carl could wait no longer, he had to have Seth's opinion.

"I'm going to listen," Seth answered.

"I am, too," Carl replied. "I have no idea why he wanted us at this meeting."

Carl immediately felt guilty. He knew the horse he saw in Marshall was the same horse that was at the barn. He didn't know if Seth had ever figured it out or had seen the horse.

After all these years, Carl wondered if the horse was still alive. He couldn't remember how long it had been since the day he saw it in Marshall. He guessed it was probably four or five years old when it was at the barn. It was now over twenty years since the shooting.

*"How long do horses live?"* Carl thought, and then was startled when he didn't know whether he had said it aloud or not.

"Carl, you ever wonder if that horse is still alive?" Seth asked. The remark startled Carl even more, and he was still wondering if he had talked out loud instead of thinking. The comment by Seth, or rather the question, was an admission to Carl that they both knew the same thing. The horse at the barn was Alan Bryant's. They'd never said it aloud until now. The question went unanswered.

Neither one of them commented any further as they continued to follow Preacher Ed, Fred Hudson, and Willie to the meeting with Alan. They would know soon enough. They had crossed two more low-water bridges and could see a colonial style house in the distance. The fields were full of Herford cattle and were well-kept. They had made it to Alan Bryant's farm.

Preacher Ed stopped his car and parked in front of the hitching rail. From looking at the ground and the lack of any sign of horses being tied to the rail, there had not been a horse tied there in a long time. Seth parked with the front of his truck close to the rail.

Carl and Seth sat in the pickup, waiting for Preacher Ed and Willie to get out first. So far there was no sign of life at the farm. Carl wasn't sure he'd ever been here before. Over the years he had gone with Willie to a lot of places to pick up livestock and deliver moonshine, but he couldn't remember being at Alan Bryant's farm.

"Have you been here before, Seth?" Carl asked.

"Yeah, me and Melissa came here to a family reunion the first year we were married, not long after the shooting," Seth answered.

They eventually all got out of their vehicles and were standing next to the hitching rail when a young man came around from the back of the house.

"I'm Leon," he introduced himself. He appeared to be a few years younger than Carl. Seth knew him. He had met him when they came for the reunion.

"Preacher Ed, you and Fred and Willie go in the house. Dad's expecting you" Leon pointed to the door as he shook hands with Preacher Ed.

Seth's mind was racing as he tried to remember the story Melissa told him about Leon. Then he remembered that Leon was what caused the trouble between Alan and Coy. He wondered if Carl knew the story about Leon being born four months after Alan returned from World War I, and it was obvious Coy Bryant was his dad. Coy had taken care of the farm for Alan while he was in Germany, but he also took care of more than the farm.

Seth started walking toward the horse corral behind the house. Leon was left standing with Carl. After introducing themselves, they caught up with Seth just as he reached the corral. Seth's mind flashed back to the day he saw the horse that left the barn the day of the shooting. It was here in this corral. In the far corner stood a horse. Leon gave a whistle, and the horse came toward them at a slow walk.

"This old horse is dad's favorite," Leon said.

Carl immediately recognized it as the horse Alan was riding in Marshall. He had been shocked as he watched Alan riding away from the courthouse. It was the same horse he saw leaving the barn the day of the shooting. Seth thought it was also the same horse he saw years earlier in the corral. The horse was old. The bright chestnut coat was now showing a lot of gray hair. The mane and tail were no longer black but were much lighter with a lot of gray hair. The horse stuck his head over the corral fence and Leon began stroking its neck.

"Fifteen years ago, he had too much fire and spirit to let me do this," Leon said as he continued stroking the horse. "Dad won't sell him for slaughter to the soap factories, I guess he'll just die here in the corral."

There was a pause before he said, "Dad wanted me to visit with you and Carl while he had a few words with Preacher Ed." Leon was nervous. "Let's go in now."

They walked away from the corral and went in the back door of the house.

# CHAPTER 11

L eon led the way into the house. Carl and Seth followed behind him. Seth paused to look at the kitchen and Carl went past him. Carl stopped to look at the guns hanging on the wall in the office next to the living room. It was the largest collection of guns he'd ever seen. There were rifles along with cases full of matching pistols. He was looking at two long barreled handguns when Leon came back and made a comment.

"I think those guns were in the family when they left England to come to North Carolina," Leon said.

"Are they for fighting duels?" Carl asked. He remembered reading a couple of stories written about the original signers of the Declaration of Independence fighting a duel. He could not remember the names of the two people who decided to fight the duel.

Leon interrupted his thoughts, "Yes, the person that chose the weapons furnished the pistols, that's how the rules of a duel were explained to me. These pistols were used in several different duels."

The conversation about the guns ended and they went into the living room. It was the largest room Carl ever remembered seeing. There was a fireplace at each end and a stairway leading to a balcony across from each fireplace. The railing and the balcony extended the entire length of the room. Carl could see four doors entering rooms off the balcony. The ceiling above the main room was the tallest he had ever seen.

They walked along underneath the balcony until they turned and went to the sitting area where Preacher Ed was standing and talking with Willie, Fred Hudson, and Alan Bryant.

"Come in, boys," Preacher Ed said as he turned and pointed toward the chairs alongside where Alan was seated. "I will sit down and let Alan explain why he wanted us here."

Preacher Ed took a chair sightly in front of Alan.

"Seth, I have met you before," Alan said. Then, turning to Carl, he added, "I know all about you—every time I've talked to Willie for the last twenty years, every story he's told me, starts with 'me and Carl'."

Everybody laughed for the first time since Leon brought Carl and Seth into the room.

Carl looked around and noticed Leon was no longer in the room with them. He was surprised at how well Alan looked because he was expecting him to be on his deathbed.

Alan continued, "I want to clear something up before I tell you why I wanted you here. That was my horse at Coy's barn when the shooting occurred." He looked at everybody for a second before he continued, "I did not do the shooting; I was in Oklahoma working."

Several minutes passed before Alan said anything else.

"Carl, I was with your dad, Tom, in Oklahoma," Alan added.

Carl was shocked. It was the first time he had ever heard

anything about where his dad was. He didn't know why his family never kept in touch with him after they left for Oklahoma. If Willie knew his dad was working in the same area as Alan Bryant, he never mentioned it.

"My doctors don't give me much chance of living much longer. I am having a good day today, but I'm glad we were not meeting earlier this week." Alan stood up, went across the room, and got a glass of water. After sitting back down he said. "This is going to be a long story."

He began to tell how the shooting happened. He went into considerable background information about after Tom got to Oklahoma. He went to Big Flat to Jim Rhodes's store.

"Jim told me he knew about his wife, Ruth, and Coy. She's meeting Coy every chance they get; Fred Hudson caught them in Coy's barn and Preacher Ed came upon her and Coy in a glade down on Spring Creek.'' Alan went on to explain that Jim didn't have a plan to do anything about it. "I asked Jim why he was telling me this."

Alan looked around to see if Leon had left the room before continuing.

"I know all of you know the story about Leon being born four months after I returned from the war," He paused, taking a drink of water, and then he said, "I chose to forgive my wife, I also decided to never be in Coy's presence again".

He took the glass back to the kitchen.

"I have a reason for wanting to clear this up. Seth, I saw the expression on your face when you saw my stud horse." Seth's face turned red, but he didn't comment. ''I didn't know for sure if the horse had been at the barn, but I knew you were a witness and you had told Sheriff Joe Carson you saw the horse and rider."

"Carl, I saw your expression when you saw me riding the horse in Marshall.'' Alan turned to Carl. "I don't want to die without everyone understanding how this happened.'' Alan began a long dissertation about the circumstances that led to the shooting.

"When I got back from visiting with Jim Rhodes, I told Tom Harris—your dad, Carl—about the conversation with Jim."

Everybody was looking baffled, trying to make sense of the story, and it was taking Alan a long time to get started telling it. He began an explanation about how he and Tom continuously talked about Coy. They were living in a tent on a drilling site and one of the workers staying with them was a rugged cowboy from Montana.

They would spend a great deal of time talking about how Coy Bryant ought to be shot. He and Tom began to talk about how easy it would be to hide in Coy's barn and do the shooting. Chad Ogden was the cowboy. He would listen intently.

"I even went into details with Tom about how easy it would be to hide your horse in the little stable on the back of the barn" Alan began to describe the barn. "We all built the same barn plan. I've got two of them here on this place. There's three, I think, on Coy's land." Alan paused for a second. "Willie, you built the same barn at the bridge, didn't you?"

"Yeah, you know I did. I came to you, and you gave me the dimensions and I looked at your barn before I started mine." Willie confirmed.

He went on to explain how it became an obsession for him and Tom to complain and plot against Coy because he ruined their lives.

"I know when Tom lost the four heifers, and after his wife died, he became soured toward Coy Bryant as bad as I was after coming home to a pregnant wife." Alan's face flushed as he became angry just telling the story.

Preacher Ed interrupted, "Alan, can I get a drink of water?''

"Sure. All of you get a drink, and let's visit about

something else for a minute," Alan replied.

Seth left the room. Carl followed him. They went to the porch. Seth stretched his arms up, holding onto the beam which supported the deck above. There were two levels to the front porches. They were identical with posts supporting the roof system extending from the upper deck. The railing had ballast close together and the railing above and below the ballast was six inches wide. Carl looked at the paint. It was in good shape and was white.

"I don't know if it would be worth it to have a porch and railings like this if you had to paint it," Seth said as he stood still, watching Carl inspect the porch.

Carl nodded in agreement. He would hate having a porch with the maintenance and all the painting of the ballast. Discussion of the porch was a distraction they were using while their thoughts were on the discussion they had been listening to inside. Carl's eyes left the porch. He was looking at Seth when he returned to the discussion of Allan's horse.

"We have known all these years that the horse at the barn was Alan's stud," Seth interrupted his own thought about the porch.

"Yeah, I thought you knew more than you ever said," Carl responded.

"When you recognized the horse in Marshall, was there any way you could tell anyone?" Seth asked.

"No, what good would it have done for us to tell anyone we knew it was Alan Bryant's horse?"

The conversation ended when Willie came and told them Alan wanted to continue his story.

# CHAPTER 12

Carl and Seth followed Willie back into the main room of the house.

Alan asked them to sit closer to him, where he would not need to talk as loud.

"I'm getting tired, and I want to finish telling everything about what happened before and after the shooting at the barn." Alan cleared his throat and took a deep breath after saying that.

"I was home sometime in July before the shooting that fall," he continued, looking directly at Carl while he was talking. "I saw Jim Rhodes in Marshall. He told me he went to the train depot at Sylamore on Tuesdays to check off the supplies at the train depot before they were delivered to Big Flat. He was hiring two wagons to transport the supplies from the train depot to his store. He had to go check them and make sure of how they were loaded because he had been getting damaged goods and couldn't prove whose fault it was, the railroad company or the wagons hauling the stuff after it left the train." Alan took a breath and rested.

Seth thought, *this is going to take forever, if he has to give us every detail that's not related to the story.*

He looked at Carl, and Carl looked back with a smile that told Seth he was thinking the same thing.

Alan must've sensed their thoughts. "I apologize, I didn't need to give you all the details of why Jim was going to the train depot. He told me after he found out Ruth was seeing Coy, he realized she was going to meet him at the barn on the day that he went to Sylamore. When I got back to Oklahoma, Tom and I continued our obsession about putting a stop to Coy Bryant's philandering with women and just stealing from whomever he could."

Alan took another pause and a drink of water before he continued. "I went into every detail of how I could ride my horse to the barn and get there in the early morning. I could go into the back stall and cover my horse with blinders." Alan turned to Willie. "Willie, I could hunt ducks on Buffalo River and ride that horse up behind a drift and cover his head and he wouldn't make a sound; I could sit there and if another horse rode down the river he wouldn't snicker. I could shoot the ducks and he wouldn't even flinch."

Alan's tone when he described the horse was that of a proud owner of a well-trained Chestnut colored stud.

"I had all these discussions with Tom Harris at night, and Chad Ogden just sat and listened. He never asked a question; I went into every detail about how far it was from my house and the route I would take to get to Coy's barn. This talk went on for maybe a month." Alan stopped again and walked a few steps from his chair. He stretched his arms and before anyone could get up.

"I needed to do that. Let me continue," he said, and sat back down. "Sometime in the fall, Chad had sent some telegrams to a farmer over on White River about buying several Hereford cattle. He told me he needed to know how he could get a wrangler to help him put these cattle in the stockyard at the depot at Flippin. He said if I had one good horse and a couple men to help me, I could manage the cattle." Alan stopped again, took a couple of sips of water, and continued. "I made a deal with him that he could use my horse and he agreed to buy a couple of bulls I had for sale. I never thought any more about it. He left. He caught the train in Yukon, Oklahoma and told me he would probably be gone in over a month. He was taking the cattle to his and his brothers ranch in Montana."

Alan Bryant's expression became very serious. "The next thing I got was a telegram telling me Coy had been killed and a woman was with him. I had no idea it was our cousin Jim Rhodes's wife. I had no idea that my horse was involved, and the shooter had used the plan Tom Harris and I discussed."

Carl looked around the room. Preacher Ed, Fred Hudson and Willie were sitting listening in disbelief. Seth had the same curious look on his face he'd had ever since Alan started the story by directing his comments to Seth and Carl, telling them he knew they had seen his horse.

"I didn't choose to come home for the funeral. I didn't know any details, but when I came home, Sheriff Joe Carson came to see me. He wanted to know where I was, and I think it was because everyone knew the details about my grudge toward my brother. I don't have any excuses for the hatred I was expressing about Coy to Tom Harris. The hardest thing in my life has been to raise Leon as my son, knowing my brother is his biological father. It ruined family reunions. My mother was still alive and living here when Leon was conceived. She told me she just thought Coy was being protective and doing a great job looking after the farm while I was in Europe.'' Alan Bryant's face showed the emotion and hurt he was expressing.

He paused once again. "I'll try to finish the story. Chad Ogden owed me $3,800 for the bulls. That was a lot of money in the 1920s. He never sent me any money. About a month after the shooting, I got a telegram in Yukon, Oklahoma, from somewhere west of Sydney, Montana. I forgot the name of the ranch. It simply said, and I quote, 'I solved your problem, thanks for the bulls.'

Alan took several drinks of water, leaned back in his chair and closed his eyes for a few minutes.

Nobody, including Preacher Ed, said anything. They thought that was probably the end of the story, but it wasn't.

"I got a letter from Montana three weeks ago. It was from Chad Ogden's widow. The main line in the letter said that Chad left a note to his wife instructing that when he died she was write a letter to Alan Bryant telling him he could tell the whole story about the shooting and that he did it on his own. He explained he did it because growing up in Texas, "we shot people like Coy Bryant. When I listened to Alan and Tom Harris talk about Coy, I thought, *why don't somebody shoot the sucker?'* That's the end of the story."

Everybody started to talk about what it was. Preacher Ed waited until Willie finished with what he thought, and then he took the floor.

"Hatred is a terrible thing. It's been with us since its creation. Alan, I don't know how you feel. The result of hatred is always a tragedy. We've spent the last twenty years guessing about the shooting. Willie and I questioned ourselves about how this was possible. You just explained the mystery. I'm not going to try to assess who's at fault. I think legally the shooting's over, and I think we forget it." Preacher Ed went down on one knee.

Carl assumed the preacher prayed for Alan. Carl and Seth, along with Willie and Fred Hudson, didn't say anything, but when Preacher Ed stood up, he said, "Gentlemen, I need to start back to Big Flat."

# CHAPTER 13

Seth and Carl were able to keep up with Preacher Ed as they started back. They sat silently. They could see Willie in the back of Preacher Ed's car, and he seemed to be gesturing as he talked.

Carl was trying to absorb all the conversation at Alan Bryant's house. After twenty plus years they had finally listened to the details of the shooting. It would be wrong to add anything to the story.

"Carl, can you believe how accurate Preacher Ed and Willie's theory of the shooting turned out to be?" Seth asked.

"No, that's the hard part for me to reconcile—the description Willie gave about believing the shooter had hidden a horse in the back stable and waited for Coy and the woman to show up," Carl answered.

They were quiet again. Preacher Ed pulled off the road in front of the St. Joe Mercantile. Willie got out of the backseat of Preacher Ed's car and came back to Seth's truck.

"We want another one of them cokes," Willie said. All five of them went silently into the Mercantile and got cokes from the Coca-Cola icebox. There was no conversation while they drank their cokes. It was like they were stunned by the information Alan had shared.

They were back on the road in no time, and once again Preacher Ed was driving fast on the pavement of Highway 65.

Seth began to wonder why Alan Bryant chose to meet with them. After all these years the discussion had ended. There was no logical reason to bring it up now.

Had he heard people accusing him of being the shooter? Was he convinced that he needed to explain because he knew that Seth and Carl had recognized his horse?

Carl sat quietly and did not interrupt Seth and his thought process.

"Are you going to say anything about what we heard on this trip?" Seth asked.

"I can't think of a good reason to tell it, or anybody who needs to know it," Carl finally answered.

"I think the same thing. Are we going to tell our wives?" Seth sounded sure when he asked the question.

"We'll have to tell them something or they're going to be questioning us for a long time," Carl said.

"Let's just tell them the bare facts. We both knew it was Alan's horse at the barn and he realized we knew it, and that was the reason he invited us to come see him." Seth paused before he continued. "We'll have to tell them who the shooter was in those circumstances."

Carl didn't answer. He spent the next few minutes trying to think whether they would ask their wives to keep it secret. He finally decided what he thought they should do.

"I believe we just tell them the whole story. I don't think we ask them to keep it a secret. Alan Bryant did not ask us not to tell. I believe he wants the story out and doesn't care who knows." Carl sat quietly, waiting for Seth to answer.

Seth sped back up, trying to catch up with Preacher Ed. During the time they had their conversation about whether to tell their wives, they had fallen behind Preacher Ed's car. They saw him turn the curve going up the hill past the Buffalo River bridge. He didn't answer Carl until he was directly behind the preacher's car.

"I think you're right," Seth commented. "I still don't think we should have talked about recognizing the horse. There were too many details that we could not fill in."

Seth had to shift gears as they came up the hill from the Buffalo River. After the car made the top of the hill, he shifted back to a higher gear. Preacher Ed was still driving faster than Seth liked to drive.

"I don't believe anything will come of it. The shooter is dead. While Alan Bryant and your dad may have caused that feller to do the shooting, I still can't believe he did." Seth turned and faced Carl, taking his eyes off the road. "He kept Alan's money, and, in a sense, it became a murder for hire."

"I don't want to be caught up in any more discussion about the shooting." Carl sounded disgusted.

"I feel the same way." Seth had to slow down. For some reason, Preacher Ed was driving much slower.

The conversation stopped when they realized the reason for Preacher Ed slowing down was that there were several goats loose in the road. A truck was parked on the side of the road. There were several people out trying to get the goats off the road. Seth pulled in behind the preacher's car and they joined the folks trying to clear the highway of the goats.

"Maybe that's what we needed for a break from what we just learned about the shooting," Carl said after they were back in the car and the goats were off the road," I have never told anyone that I thought it was Alan's horse at the barn;"

"I've not told anyone." Once again, Seth sounded irritated.

They went into a lengthy discussion about their responsibilities after they realized the horse belonged to Alan Bryant.

"How could we tell anybody? There's a lot of details that needed to go with the fact we recognized a horse," Carl asked Seth.

"That is the truth of it," Seth continued to express how he felt. "Sheriff Joe Carson came to see me a few days after the shooting. I did not show him where I was standing when I saw the horse and rider go up the hill. Because I didn't see it well enough to know for sure who it was, nor if had I ever seen the horse before."

"I was the same way. When the shots were fired the mules turned and ran with the wagon. I saw the horse and rider as they went over the hill away from the barn. I'm not sure where I was when I saw them. It may have been as the mules were turning and stampeding, or it may have been after I got them under control and drove back to the barn." Carl's description took some time for him to complete.

# CHAPTER 14

They rode in silence. Preacher Ed was driving slower through the curves just north of Marshall. Carl and Seth would be following them until they got to the junction at Hickory Hollow. They could see Willie still leaning forward toward the front of the car and gesturing with his hands at times.

"I wonder what they're saying now about the visit with Alan," Seth was curious about their opinion.

"I don't want to know what they are saying," Carl answered. His voice showed signs of irritation and he didn't say anymore as he waited for Seth to reply and hoped they could drop the subject.

"I'm tired of it, too," Seth added solemnly.

"You know you're right, Carl. Even if we don't want to continue this discussion, we'll have to tell our wives about the details Alan Bryant gave us about the shooting." Seth stopped in his conversation for a minute.

"Let's not give any information about when we saw Alan Bryant's horse and why we were sure it was the horse that was at the barn. I am tired of this—after twenty years, I was ready to forget it" Carl replied.

They were not able to drop the discussion as they followed Preacher Ed, Willie, and Fred Hudson on the gravel road from Marshall to Hickory Hollow. They continued to guess about the story Alan Bryant told. Was it possible for it to be true? How could a cowboy that grew up in Texas get to Arkansas and find the barn and sit there waiting to shoot someone? How could he become concerned enough listening to Alan Bryant and Tom Harris to do what he did?

While they bantered back and forth with each one offering a question and a theory, they never reached a conclusion.

"This is unbelievable how close Preacher Ed and Willie's theories were about the shooting," Seth said.

Carl didn't tell him he had listened while he was cleaning harness to Preacher Ed and Willie as they discussed the shooting with him. They made it to the junction at Hickory Hollow. Carl was glad the trip was over, but he'd really enjoyed spending the time with Seth. They both got out and walked toward Preacher Ed's car. The preacher did not get out of his car; he was ready to get back to Big Flat.

Carl shook hands with Seth and told him how much he enjoyed spending the day with him.

"Don't breathe a word of our discussion with anybody until after we talk to our wives," Seth whispered as he shook Carl's hand.

Carl traded places with Fred Hudson and watched as Fred and Seth pulled away heading toward Rock Creek. He got in the car with Preacher Ed and Willie without saying anything.

"It's been a long day," Preacher Ed commented as they started down the hill toward the Big Creek bridge.

"Long is not the word for it," Willie answered.

Carl did not say a word. He did not want to get into a discussion. Preacher Ed did not stop at Willie's house. He drove past and went on to the barn. He stopped next to the hitching rail and got out and started toward the barn. Willie followed. Carl watched the two friends as they entered the poker room where they drank moonshine for years. He followed them in.

Without asking, Willie took three cups off their hangers. The sun was beginning to set. It had been a long, hot day, and Carl wondered if drinking a toddy was a good idea. Willie poured moonshine into each cup. It was the good stuff. Carl watched as Willie handed Preacher Ed his cup. Willie picked up his cup and left Carl's sitting on the poker table. They both sat down. Carl finally picked up his cup of moonshine. No one had spoken yet.

"Did you and Seth actually see Alan Bryant's stud at the barn the day of the shooting?" Willie asked.

"We have never identified the shooter, and Alan Bryant admitted his horse was at the barn." Carl was being careful with what he said. He was trying to remember the conversation at Alan Bryant's house.

"It's over, it's time we move on, the shooter is dead. Alan Bryant is not going to live much longer and there's no point in discussing something when there's no solution," Preacher Ed spoke up for the first time.

They drank in silence. Carl had never sat down. He shook hands with Preacher Ed without saying anything, and nodded his head at Willie as he left the barn.

Carl started to walk home. The dusk had not arrived, but the shadows were becoming deeper. He was going to make it home before dark. He wondered if Pauline would have his supper cooked. He stopped on the rocks for the creek crossing and stood and watched the water swirling between the rocks. It was dry. Big Creek was low as usual for July. The swimming hole above the bridge was a center of activity every day. Farmers came with their bars of soap and used the creek to take a bath. The kids came with them and played in the water.

Today was not wasted. Carl walked home and looked back as he climbed the hill toward his house. He wondered how long Preacher Ed and Willie would stay at the barn. He didn't want to get involved in any more questions. He had been totally surprised when Preacher Ed brought Jim Rhodes's letter, and they all agreed to go see Alan Bryant. Answers? What good were they now? He finished climbing the hill and opened the door to his house.

"You've been gone all day," Pauline commented.

She gave Carl a hug. The frown she had on her face told Carl she smelled the moonshine.

"You went with daddy and Preacher Ed?" Her voice was questioning, but Carl knew she knew the answer.

He didn't answer. He looked at the table, and his plate was in its usual place. He sat down without saying a word, and Pauline got him a glass of iced tea.

He began eating. Pauline sat on his left, as usual from the day he arrived at the bridge. He began to think back over his conversation with Seth. They had agreed to tell their wives everything. Carl began telling the story. He wasn't sure if he embellished it or if he said it accurately. He watched Pauline's face as he told the story of his dad sitting in the tent with Alan Bryant. She never stepped in and asked any questions, she just listened.

Carl finished the story.

"What now?" was Pauline's only comment.

"Me and Seth agreed to tell you and Melissa the whole story. I'm not asking you to keep it a secret. Seth is not going to ask Melissa to either. I just don't think it's anything we need to continue discussing," Carl finally answered.

They sat on the porch facing Big Creek. The shadows had turned to dusk. You could hear the whippoorwill calling from behind the house on the top of the hill. You could hear another one answering somewhere up Hickory Hollow. The same places they always seem to spend their nights calling out to each other. The lightning bugs you could see were many between them and Big Creek. It was peaceful. Pauline stood up. She took Carl by the hand, and they went inside. The story was not going to interfere with their lives.

# CHAPTER 15

The end of September 1944 was colder than usual. A killing frost was rare on Big Creek before the first of October. The cane was stripped and ready for making sorghum, but Willie Sitton didn't have his usual enthusiasm. It'd been over two months since the trip to see Alan Bryant. Jim Rhodes came by the barn and told Willie they were expecting Alan to die at any time. Willie believed that it had been two weeks ago. He was not sure.

He stood quietly, watching the water flow through the swimming hole above the bridge. As usual, the sycamore leaves were floating on top of the water and casting their shadows beneath them. Ever since he was a boy, Willie had enjoyed watching the leaves float after the first frost. He liked to find the shadow of the leaf on the bottom and follow it as the leaf moved along. There were times the floating leaf seemed to be moving slower than the shadow on the rock bottom. He'd wondered all his life if it was a trick of sunlight on the water.

Willie was waiting for Carl at the barn. He was

supposed to be there early to take him to Jim Rhodes's store in Big Flat. Willie had decided to walk along the creek while listening for Carl's automobile to arrive at the barn.The car was parked across the creek from Carl and Pauline's house. There was a hay shed on one side and a stall for the car on the other. It would be a lot of trouble to create a crossing for the car and a road to Carl and Pauline's house.

Willie heard the car start and began walking back to the barn.

"You ready to go?" Carl asked as he got out of the car in front of the blacksmith shop.

"Yeah, you're late." Willie's voice sounded irritable.

"Pauline cooked too much breakfast," Carl answered as he returned to the car.

Willie got in the car and sat down without commenting about Pauline's cooking. Carl pulled onto the bridge and the rattling of all the loose boards was louder than the sound of the engine.

"That bunch that takes care of the bridge needs to get back out here," Willie said in the same irritated tone as before. "they've got a bunch of loose boards to tighten,"

They crossed the bridge and climbed the hill to the Cedar Creek schoolhouse. Willie still hadn't said anything after the comment about the bridge. Carl was trying to figure out the reason for the trip to Big Flat. Willie had said he needed to go talk to Jim Rhodes. There had been hardly any conversation in the last two months after going to see Alan Bryant. Carl and Seth had not discussed it any further after they told Pauline and Melissa about the trip.

"I hate these automobiles. Me and Ellen were taking the buggy and going to Firestone's store at Hickory, and as I was going up the hill above the house there a car almost ran over us. He was trying to get enough speed to go up that hill without changing gears. When he rounded the curve, our buggy was in the road and there was a car coming down the hill. Caused my horse to almost run away. He slid up behind us and the car coming down the hill barely missed all of us." Willie paused. Carl had listened to his tone get stronger as he told the story of the automobile almost hitting his buggy. "And, Carl, I think I'm too old to try to learn to drive. I know cars are the best way to travel along better roads. But try taking this automobile over to Huckabee's old place. Or try to go down and see Cal Morrow. You know Sheriff Joe Carson, years ago, drove his car out where Davis Creek and Long Creek come together to make up Big Creek. He kept a horse there at Harv Brown's farm and he would ride the horse to wherever he needed to go. I know that the automobile is the way to travel in the future. But I still would rather take my buggy and drive it when Ellen and I are going somewhere. I didn't want to take the chance of driving it to Big Flat today." Willie stopped for a minute. "I want to go see Jim Rhodes; I've never told him about our conversation with Alan."

Willie stopped talking. Carl still hadn't commented. He was wondering why Willie was making the trip to Big Flat and he was wondering if Willie was trying to decide about owning an automobile. Willie was born in 1868. It was September 1944. He was seventy-six years old. Carl sat thinking about all the change Willie had seen in his life. Moonshine, sorghum, and all the things he had done to make a living were changing. His life had never been about money. The things he taught Carl from the beginning had served them well. Carl wondered if Preacher Ed would be waiting at Big Flat.

They made the rest of the trip without any conversation. When they pulled into the parking space by Jim Rhodes's store, Preacher Ed was standing in front of the main door. Carl wondered if it was a planned meeting.

# CHAPTER 16

C arl sat down on the bench in front of the store. Willie and Preacher Ed were talking about twenty feet from him. He could not hear the conversation. Carl had no interest in trying to participate. He watched as a mixture of horse-drawn wagons and automobiles came to Big Flat. Some of the horses were not startled by the automobiles, while others almost panicked.

The last few years have been traumatic for the people in the area. When the draft for World War II was implemented, a lot of people did not answer their notice, while others volunteered and were anxious to participate and protect their country. Preacher Ed's son was one of the volunteers. Carl remembered attending the funeral at the cemetery in Big Flat when Noah Tice's body arrived from Fort Dix, New Jersey. The honor guard firing their rifles into the air, while the flag-draped coffin sat ready to be lowered into the ground, was a memory that stood out. It wasn't many months until Carl and Pauline stood next to Seth and Melissa while Liz Tice was buried next to her son.

Carl wasn't aware that a little girl had been buried years earlier.

There were two boys having a scuffle a few yards away from the crowd. They went unnoticed until one of the mothers decided to break it up. Carl watched as another mother joined in the argument.

"You stay out of that!" the second mother yelled. " Your boy started it, and my boy is finishing it!"

In a matter of minutes, two families were engaged in a shoving and cursing match while the rest of the people formed a circle around the dispute.

Willie came out. When he looked at the skirmish, he commented "A normal day in Big Flat."

Without answering, Carl followed him inside where Preacher Ed and Jim Rhodes were sitting in the area where the barber chair was located. Preacher Ed had stopped cutting hair several years before. The area had now become a visiting area for men while their wives did some shopping.

"Me and Preacher Ed have been telling Jim about what Alan said when we went to his house" Willie was speaking to Carl.

"Carl, I don't see anything being accomplished about all this conversation now" Jim Rhodes said. It was the first time Carl remembered Jim Rhodes addressing him directly.

Without allowing time for Carl to answer, Preacher Ed spoke up.

"The only thing it will accomplish is to clear the air after all these years and to remove any doubt about who is guilty of the shooting," the preacher commented.

During the next few minutes, Willie and Preacher Ed took turns giving their opinion on all the discussions during the time immediately after the shooting and the trip to see Alan Bryant. Carl did not enter an opinion, nor try to contribute to the conversation.

After a couple of hours, Willie was ready to go back to

Big Creek. Carl listened as Willie greeted everybody they met. The common question was the men pulling Willie aside and asking if he was still making any moonshine.

"Not any to sell," Carl overheard Willie answer. He thought about the three or four batches a year they had made for the last few years. The still was in good shape. Every time they went to mix mash, the barrels were left unharmed and were still turned upside down and clean. Carl was always amazed how it seemed no one would bother anything that belonged to Willie Sitton.

He remembered hearing stories after he married Pauline about people making a deed for Willie and leaving the country.

"If you owe Willie and don't pay, or if he thinks you have mistreated a neighbor, your days along Big Creek are going to be short," was a common statement. Carl always wondered how those things were accomplished. He never heard of a beating, nor did he ever hear of any other violence against anyone. He couldn't answer that question in his mind.

"They don't think Alan is gonna live but a few more days," Willie commented after they were in the car and on their way home.

# CHAPTER 17

C arl pulled off the road and turned toward cozy. He immediately turned left and pulled toward the Rock Creek schoolhouse and Cemetery. The sun was barely above the treetops. For the second week in October, it was a cool morning. There had been three or four light frosts since the first one.

"Why are we leaving so early?" Pauline asked as soon as his car stopped.

"I don't know," Carl answered. "They're burying him somewhere across Buffalo River and back toward Maumee, I think," He was disgusted at having to go to the funeral, but Willie insisted. It was Alan Bryant's funeral, and Willie respected his Bryant cousins.

Carl and Pauline were in their car and waiting for Seth and Melissa to join them. They were going to ride in Carl and Pauline's car and follow Preacher Ed and Jim Rhodes, who were coming with Willie and Ellen. The plan was for them to follow Preacher Ed's car.

"Reckon why they didn't bury Alan here?" Pauline

asked after the car stopped.

"I bet it's because Coy Bryant is buried here," Carl answered.

Over the years, everyone heard the story about Coy fathering a child with Alan's wife while he was in the military. Pauline did not respond to the comment. Willie had scolded her for asking questions after the murder, when Melissa told her about Leon Bryant being the son of his uncle rather than Alan, and it might be the reason for the shooting.

The sun was now shining brightly and coming in over the line of trees behind the Rock Creek schoolhouse.

"Is there a cemetery next to all the schoolhouses?" Pauline asked.

"You know there's not. There's not one at Cozy, there's not one next to Cedar Grove," Carl responded, wondering why Pauline would ask a question when she knew the answer.

They saw Preacher Ed's car coming around the curve and approaching the schoolhouse. There still wasn't any sign of Seth and Melissa. Carl had no idea how long it was going to take to cross the ferry at the Buffalo River and find their way to the cemetery. He understood the funeral service was scheduled for 10 o'clock. It was almost 8 o'clock. He stopped worrying when he realized Preacher Ed was in charge of the funeral and it wouldn't start until they got there.

It had been less than a half hour after Preacher Ed arrived, until Seth and Melissa joined them. They were now in a line waiting to cross the Dillard ferry at the Buffalo River.

"I don't like crossing this thing," Melissa said from the backseat.

They watched as the man cranked the gearbox and the winch pulled the end of the ferry boat up the river. Carl liked to watch the ferryboat operate. The cable stretching across the river controlled the ferry and kept it from floating downstream. By swinging one end upstream, the water would push the ferry across the river. By cranking the winch for the pull cable, the operator of the ferry controlled the boat and could send it in the direction he chose. After he got started up across the river, he would straighten the boat up by releasing the cable, and the boat would land with the apron in the road. The apron was the ramp for loading and unloading the ferry. There was an apron on each end, and they also were controlled with cables.

''I can't believe that fella can get those mules to pull that wagon onto the ferry," Seth said as they watched a team of mules start onto the ramp. They did not hesitate. The driver seemed to be confident they were going to be okay. After the mules pulled the wagon on to the ferry, it was Preacher Ed's turn. He hit the ramp too hard with his car and the rear tires spun as he went on to the ferry. The operator shoveled gravel back next to the ramp before he motioned for Carl to pull onto the ferry.

Finally, they were on the ferry and crossing the river. Leaving the ferry was uneventful. Melissa was irritable and said she was becoming carsick from riding in the back of the car.

"Carl, stop and I'll get back there," Seth said. They all laughed after they started again and were trying to catch back up with Preacher Ed. It was now Carl and Melissa in the front, with Seth and Pauline riding in the back.

"We will look funny when we get to the funeral," Pauline said. "Folks that don't know us will think I'm married to Seth and you're with Melissa."

They all continued to laugh as a car ran faster along the ridges north of the Buffalo River. The gravel road was better than it was from Big Creek to the Buffalo River. They were now directly behind Preacher Ed again.

"Can you give us directions to the Caney Cemetery?"

Willie asked the farmer working next to the road on a fence.

Carl pulled close enough to hear the question.

They listened as the farmer pointed and explained how far it was to the cemetery.

"I don't believe we're going to make it in time," Seth commented as they began their journey again.

They followed the instructions given by the farmer and could see the building come into view with the cemetery behind it. The hearse was already parked, and there was a crowd gathering.

Carl followed Preacher Ed and parked beside him. They were at the funeral. Seth helped Melissa out of the car, and Pauline took Carl's hand and they walked together through the cemetery gate. It was not a funeral they looked forward to attending, but when Willie asked them to do something, they always tried to do it.

# CHAPTER 18

C arl and Pauline caught up with Willie and Ellen. They were walking toward a covered pavilion with benches for seats and a speaker's podium in the front. Carl did not see a coffin. Glancing to the right farther down into the cemetery, there was a canopy covering what looked like a gravesite.

Willie sat down on the end of the bench, letting Ellen pass in front of him and sit beside him. Carl and Pauline started to go to the other end of the same bench but decided to sit with Seth and Melissa directly behind them.

They did not see Preacher Ed and had lost track of him. He returned from the gravesite with Leon and Alan Bryant's widow. Nobody was talking. Pauline wasn't even whispering as she usually did. It was cool underneath the canopy, and they all scooted closer together trying to stay warm. Melissa leaned out and whispered to Carl.

"You have any idea how this funeral is going to be conducted?" she asked.

Before Carl could answer, Preacher Ed stepped to the

podium and said, "Let us pray."

The funeral finished. They were walking towards the cars. Carl had wondered while they were standing around the grave after the coffin was lowered if this was the end of all the questions concerning the shooting of Coy Bryant and Jim Rhodes's wife. He glanced at Seth during the graveside portion and thought from the expression on Seth's face that he was probably thinking the same thing.

Leon Bryant had read the obituary immediately after Preacher Ed finished praying. He went back and sat by his mother during the remarks Preacher Ed made. It had been a typical funeral. The things said were basically the same thing Carl had heard at every funeral he'd attended. The only thing different was that there was no praise for how great a man Alan Bryant had been.

During the graveside, Carl wondered about one remark.

"Ashes to ashes and dust to dust symbolizes the end of a life. As we gather today, we are at the end not only of a life but of an era," Preacher Ed said with a different tone than anything else he had said.

"You go ahead and ride up front with Carl," Pauline said to Melissa when they got to the car.

"I kind of liked riding in the back with Seth," she added with a laugh.

They pulled away from the parking lot without making any other comment. Preacher Ed, Willie, Ellen, and Jim Rhodes were still standing in the cemetery. Carl couldn't see who they were visiting with before they left the cemetery. He was sure they could find their way back to the ferry at Buffalo River. It was getting cooler as the day was getting well past noon.

"We have not eaten a bite since we left Rock Creek," Melissa said.

"I think that little store where we turned to come out to the cemetery will probably make us some sandwiches," Seth answered.

"You know, I thought—" Pauline stopped before concluding, "I thought there'd be food there"

Carl was listening and had not entered any of the discussion, but at the same time, he'd wondered why there wasn't more singing and why there wasn't any food at the funeral.

They dropped the subject and stopped at the little grocery. There was a gas pump that still operated with a hand pump and with the numbers for the gallons inside the glass tank. Carl looked at the pump and decided he would pump five gallons of gas.

He went into the store and asked the storekeeper to unlock the gas pump.

"How many gallons you want?" the storekeeper asked.

"Five," Carl replied.

Carl watched as the gasoline flowed into the holding tank made of glass. The tank began to fill up and as the red liquid passed each number the storekeeper would slow down the pump until he got to five. He pumped an extra lick and was slightly over the 5-gallon marker.

"I try to give good measure. With gasoline at twenty-two cents a gallon I need to give good measure, or it is going to get to the point nobody can afford to drive a car," the storekeeper said as he handed the hose to Carl for him to put the gas in the car.

They decided to sit on the bench and picnic table underneath the shade tree. The baloney was sliced thick on the sandwiches and the bread seemed to be fresh, but the cheese was thin and tasted old.

They ate in silence. Carl and Seth were drinking their usual Coca-Cola in bottles. Pauline and Melissa were drinking the new Nesbitt fruit-flavored drinks. Pauline's was a grape soda while Melissa's was an orange.

There still was no mention of any of the conversation at Alan Bryant's house in July. Carl wondered if anyone was thinking about beside him. He got his answer.

"Do you think this is the end of the discussion about who shot Coy and Jim Rhodes's wife?" Melissa asked the question.

Carl did not volunteer to answer. Seth didn't, either. Pauline looked at them before she spoke.

"I hope so," Pauline said. "I've wondered how you guys managed to keep your mouth shut for over twenty years."

Seth laughed. Carl looked at Seth and then back at Pauline and Melissa.

"When you think something, and when you couldn't possibly know it for sure, it's better to keep your mouth shut," Carl said, and then added, "Who would want to start something that would create a bunch of questions and no answers?"

Without any further discussion or comments, they got in the car and started toward Rock Creek. They still had to cross the ferry at Buffalo River. They were tired. There wasn't any discussion while they watched the ferry coming toward them. It was a load of logs, and the weight of the truck and logs prevented the ferry from coming up the ramp far enough for the car to get on the boat. When they lowered the aprons, the incline was too steep for the car to get on the boat.

They watched as the ferry operator raised the aprons up and used a pole to push the ferryboat farther up the ramp.

"It's a lot of work to operate a ferryboat," Seth commented as they pulled down to the ferry.

Climbing the hill from the Buffalo River toward Rock Creek was the steepest incline they had encountered during the entire trip. Carl watched as steam began to come out around the radiator cap. It was the first time the car had shown any sign of overheating. It was October, and this usually didn't happen on a day that was cool.

He stopped at the top of the hill and sat there for a minute, waiting for the engine to cool down, hoping the steam would stop coming out from around the radiator cap.

He would not touch the radiator cap while the engine was hot. A man at Big Flat was scalded from his face to his waist when he removed the radiator cap from an overheated vehicle.

"It's about time we trade this car," Pauline spoke up from the back seat.

Carl was too tired to get into the discussion. Neither Seth nor Melissa expressed an opinion.

After the engine cooled a little, Carl took the gallon of water from the rumble seat and removed the radiator cap and added the water. The car started. There were no more problems until they pulled in at the Rock Creek Cemetery and Melissa and Seth left to go home.

The day was over. Carl was relieved. He knew Alan Bryant was Willie's cousin. He was Melissa's uncle, and they were expected to go to the funeral. But with all the circumstances and the conversations over the years, it was a hard event for Carl to attend.

# CHAPTER 19

The winter of 1944 and spring of '45 was a little warmer than usual. World War II seemed to be ending. Troops were marching toward Germany, and Italy was no longer an aggressor. Along Big Creek, the war was no longer a topic of discussion. The renewal of the discussion about the shootings, caused by Alan Bryant's wish to see Seth Tabor and Carl Harris, caused another round of discussion, but after Alan's funeral, there hadn't been anything else said.

Carl was cranking the bellows while Willie held the plow point in the forage. Willie no longer worked at the blacksmith shop by himself. All the tools he needed to sharpen this spring were being done with Carl's help. Carl cranked the bellows and swung the hammer after the tool was placed on the anvil.

Seth and Melissa had become closer friends to Carl and Pauline because of the trip to see Alan Bryant. Carl and Seth had one thing in common that caused them to become close friends. They both were drafted but failed in their physical for the army. Seth never told Carl why he was turned down, nor did Carl tell him it was because of his enlarged heart. They had been together several times when a remark would be made about them being young men and not in the war.

The wind was terrible. It was the end of February, and evidently March was going to come in like a lion. When Willie decided the plow point was hot enough to sharpen, the wind blew sparks all over the shop when he took it out of the forge. Carl watched carefully, making sure the sparks didn't start a fire. He stepped on some shavings where they sharpened handles. They were smoking, and evidently were about to flame.

"What are you doing messing around? You need to hammer the point before it gets cold!" Willie said harshly. He wasn't aware that Carl was busy making sure the fire didn't get out.

Carl started sharpening the point. He knew exactly where to hit and paused when it was time for Willie to turn the point. He could sharpen a plow point quicker than Willie ever could.

"You're good at this, boy," Willie said as he stuck the point into the water to temper it.

Carl smiled because Willie's tone was much better than when he was fussing about him not hitting the plow point quickly enough.

They didn't hear the car when it pulled into the barnyard.

"What are you fellers doing?" It was Sheriff Nick Reed. He had taken over several years before. He replaced long-serving Joe Carson. Searcy County politics were made up of a well-managed group of people. The officers that served for many years would usually select their successors.

Willie looked around and spoke to Sheriff Reed. "What are you doing in these parts today?" he asked.

Willie didn't recognize Joe Carson as he got out of the

car. He was stooped over and had lost a lot of weight since he had left the Sheriff's office. Willie recognized him after he got closer to him.

He was amazed when he saw Joe, because his eyes were level with Joe's. Willie realized he was taller. The Sheriff Joe Carson he remembered was a head taller than he was. Willie ignored Sheriff Reed and shook hands with Joe.

Carl had stood back and not greeted the sheriff or the ex-sheriff. He, too, was amazed at the change in the stature of Joe Carson. And then he realized Joe had to be older than Willie. He listened and didn't quite understand when Sheriff Nick Reed told Willie he brought Joe because Joe wanted to hear an explanation of an old case.

Willie turned to Carl and said, "Let's go inside the barn, they want to hear a story."

Carl followed as they went into the barn ahead of him. When Carl got to the barn, he was surprised; Willie was taking four cups down from where they hung on the wall.

Carl wondered if Willie was going to pour some of the last batch of moonshine they made and serve it to the sheriff. In a matter of minutes, he got his answer as Willie poured a small amount of moonshine into each cup.

"Always wanted to serve you a cup of moonshine, Joe," Willie said with a laugh as he handed a cup to the retired and current sheriffs of Searcy County, Arkansas.

Carl was left speechless. He had noticed a more carefree attitude in Willie over the last few months. Maybe it had started before Alan Bryant died, but during the winter Willie became less disciplined.

Carl picked up his cup and began to sip the liquor. It was good stuff. Willie sat down first. Carl went to the same side of the poker table and sat down next to Willie. The sheriff and the retired sheriff remained standing. Carl wondered how the conversation would start.

"You're that boy that was driving the wagon, and the first one to the barn the day of the shooting," Carson said as he leaned forward and looked at Carl as if to make sure of who he was. He then sat down closer to Willie, but on the opposite side from Carl.

Nick Reed looked confused. He continued to stand shifting from one foot to the other as if he wasn't sure he should sit down. He was holding his cup of moonshine but had not taken a drink of it.

"Well, this is different," Sheriff Reed said as he took a drink and sat down.

Carl was a little bit amazed. He just saw Willie serve moonshine to the law, and he'd seen the law take a drink without asking a question.

*"Now, what's next?"* was the thought that came into Carl's mind.

Nobody spoke for a few minutes. Then Joe Carson went into a long statement of what he had been hearing. He may have been stooped and frail compared to the broad-shouldered sheriff from years ago, but his mind was sharp.

After he finished telling them everything, he looked over at Carl and asked, "Did you have any idea that horse belonged to Alan Bryant when you saw it at the barn?"

"No," Carl answered in a sharp tone. He was irritated that those questions about the shooting seemed to be coming back again.

Sheriff Joe stopped talking. Sheriff Reed went into a long discussion about how the file had never been closed. And he went on to say that the reason they were there was to satisfy Joe Carson's curiosity about the murders and see if, as a sheriff, he had failed to do his job.

Willie took the conversation over. He reviewed everything that had been said about the conversation with Alan Bryant, and then he added, "It's over. Chad Ogden, according to Alan Bryant, was the shooter. He was able to find his way to the barn and wait for Coy Bryant and Sister Rhodes to meet. He did this based on a conversation he overheard between Alan Bryant and Tom Harris, Carl's dad. The shooter is dead. Alan Bryant is dead. There are no witnesses to testify. There's no one alive to prosecute. Close your file." Willie stood up and hung his cup back on the wall.

"Willie, you're right," Sheriff Reed said.

That was the end of the discussion about the shooting. The rest of the visit was spent with Sheriff Nick Reed getting acquainted with Carl Harris and Willie Sitton. He told how he had heard ever since he'd been a kid that Willie Sitton made the best moonshine in the area.

"I believe it now," he concluded and hung his cup alongside Willie's.

# CHAPTER 20

The hog pen below the bluff was enclosed with web wire fencing. The post next to the bluff was braced out to a timber that ran taut to the bluff. The fencing next to Hickory Hollow extended out into the gravel. The fencing in the gravel had to be kept clean of debris and repaired continuously.

As soon as Willie finished his breakfast, he told Ellen, "I am going to repair the hog pen fence today."

He was re-stapling all the areas where the hogs had managed to pull the wire loose. All the debris from last year's floods had to be removed from the fence before this year's spring rain started. Willie's grandfather, Noah Sitton, said "If we don't keep the fence clean, the first spring rain will take the fence out."

Willie ignored that one year and the debris that was caught in the fence tore the fence down. While he was repairing it, he remembered the reason his grandfather Noah gave for cleaning it out.

"When the first floodwaters come down, they are not

carrying anything with them. But all this debris gets caught in the top of the fence and settles to the bottom. Willie remembered him pausing and saying. "We clean it out, and it will be all right until the next spring." Willie never ignored cleaning out the debris after that time.

"Willie!" Someone was calling his name from the top of the bluff above the hog pen.

He did not recognize the voice until the man was coming down the trail to where he was working.

"Ellen said you were down here." It was Willie's brother-in-law, Jim Rhodes.

Jim seldom visited Willie but stopped often to see Ellen. Willie wondered why Jim would climb down the bluff where he was working on the hog pen today.

He spent the next several minutes listening to Willie explain why he had to clean and repair the fence. Jim Rhodes never made any comment, just listened. When Willie had finished with his explanation of the work, he was doing he asked Jim. "What have you got on your mind today?" Willie went straight to the point.

"Nick Reed, the Searcy County Sheriff, called me into his office when I was in Marshall yesterday," Jim Rhodes started to explain.

Willie's mind raced because he knew what was coming next. It had only been a week since the sheriff brought Joe Carson to the bridge.

"He told me about bringing old Sheriff Carson out to see you and Carl." Jim was hesitant. Willie waited while Jim walked around the entire perimeter of the hog pen and back. Willie began driving staples into the fence post securing the new piece of web wire. Finally, Jim walked up and continued.

"He asked me about the letter I got from Alan Bryant, and why he would write it to me." Jim sat down on the bank of the creek before adding, "I had to explain it all to him."

For the next several minutes, Jim Rhodes gave a complete history of his conversation with Alan Bryant over twenty-five years ago. He told how he knew when he married Ruth that she was a woman with an eye for all the men. He talked about how lonesome he was after he lost his first wife. He told about how he went to Marshall and got trapped in a snowstorm. He spent several days in a hotel just off the square.

"I knew Ruth was entertaining men in the hotel. The last night I was there, she came to my room." Jim stood up and threw a stick across the Hickory Hollow branch. It landed on the gravel bar before it bounced out of the creek bed into the woods.

"I brought her home with me to Big Flat. I didn't really care. I was lonesome. She was beautiful. She was over twenty years younger than me. She was Mrs. Jim Rhodes." He sat back down. He had not made eye contact with Willie while he was telling him the story.

He spent the next few minutes talking about how hard she worked at the store. What a good job she did with keeping the house clean and supporting him in his church work.

"The only fault I could have with her was her attraction to men." Jim took a deep breath. "The first time we saw Coy Bryant, I knew they would get together."

He went on for several minutes, telling Willie he didn't know when it started. Willie was shocked when he talked about overhearing Preacher Ed and Fred Hudson discussing Ruth and Coy meeting.

"I saw Alan a couple times after I overheard the conversation about Ruth and Coy." Jim stood back up to walk across the gravel and looked back toward the hog pen.

"I don't know why I decided to tell Alan, I have regretted that ever since the shooting. I was not going to do anything about it." Jim drew a deep breath. "I don't know how wrong it was for me to marry her in the first place. I don't know how stupid it was to put up with her." He stepped closer to Willie. "I miss her until this day, and I don't know why I've decided to tell you this. It's over, she's been dead for years. Coy was no good, but he was a cousin. I didn't want him shot, either."

Jim started to walk away. Willie watched as he went around the east end of the hog pen. He didn't go back up the path where he came down. Jim Rhodes walked slowly away with slumped shoulders and went out of Willie's sight toward Big Creek. Willie wondered why he didn't take the path. It would be almost three hundred yards to the barn before he could go back up the bluff to the house where Ellen was.

Willie went back to repairing the fence. He had to make sure there was gravel close to the bottom and he had to put the timber back down to keep the pigs from getting out. It was a good mental break to finish the repairs to the hog pen. Willie wondered if there were more stories about the shooting that he hadn't heard yet. He could smell his dinner being cooked as he got back to the house. Jim Rhodes's car was gone. He wondered if Ellen knew anything about what her brother told him. He washed his hands and got ready to eat.

# CHAPTER 21

The dinner was delicious. Ellen had cooked some fish patties. Willie always gigged suckers in December. He scraped the scales and cleaned the fish just like he was going to fry them. Instead, Ellen was using the new pressure cooker they had bought for canning. Willie had a lot of Mason jars that he didn't use for moonshine anymore, and they were sitting on the shelves full of fish.

Willie had watched one day as Ellen opened one of the jars of fully cooked fish. The bones had disintegrated during the pressure cooking, and she took the fish and mixed oats and flour along with a little bit of cornmeal and made them into patties. She would then deep fry until they were golden brown. A few fried potatoes, a little bit of sauerkraut, some sweet pickles, and Willie had what he always liked for his noon meal.

The meal started with Willie asking a question.

"Jim didn't want to stay for lunch?" he asked.

Ellen didn't answer. She handed him some relish she had made from green tomatoes, red bell peppers, and a little bit of cabbage.

"Try this relish on your fish patty, I put some on mine. It's good," Ellen said.

Willie knew she was avoiding the question, and he was afraid she would ask about his and Jim's conversation. He didn't need to worry.

"Jim told me he wanted to tell you about his conversation with Sheriff Nick Reed." Ellen began to tell Willie everything she had heard from Jim.

She told Willie that Jim thought it was his fault that Ruth got killed along with Coy. She said, "Jim said if he had kept his mouth shut and not said anything to Alan, Ruth would still be alive."

Willie couldn't answer. While he was taking his first bite of relish, a thought went through his mind.

*I can't imagine sitting in church next to a man that I knew was with my wife on Tuesday before I went to church.* Willie blushed at the thought. Ellen had said something else, but Willie missed it while he had the thought and envisioned Sister Rhodes naked with Coy.

It was time for all this discussion to end. He wondered why Alan had to bring it up again. Since July and the trip to see Alan, it had been a constant barrage of people wanting to know different things. The surprise visit by Jim Rhodes, and what he had said while he was at the hog pen, created a whole new perspective in Willie's mind.

He had always thought Jim Rhodes had no idea of what was going on with his wife. Today he had learned Jim knew from the beginning about his wife's addiction to men.

Jim Rhodes always avoided one-on-one contact with Willie because of his religion and opposition to moonshine. Preacher Ed and Willie never discussed Jim Rhodes, and they never had any negative comments about him. Jim Rhodes brought Preacher Ed to Big Flat.

Willie finished the meal and went to the shelf where his parched corn was kept. As he took the lid off to get enough kernels of corn to last for the afternoon and put them in his bib pocket, Ellen scooted the skillet back on the stove. She was going to have to parch more corn. Willie loved parched corn. It was just whole kernels of corn that were usually ground into cornmeal.

Ellen cooked them by using leftover grease and dumping the kernels in to toast them. His mother had given them to him as a snack. He started carrying them in the bib pocket so he could keep playing when he was a boy and not lose the grains of parched corn. Now, at 78 years old, he was still doing it.

He made his way to the barn. He hoped Carl would come around. He wasn't sure whether he would discuss Jim Rhodes's visits with Carl. While he was walking to the barn, he decided he wouldn't have any further discussion.

There was no need to continue to add fuel to the discussion that should have ended years ago. While Willie was totally surprised to learn how Jim Rhodes got his wife, he was equally surprised that he was tolerating her behavior. There was no way he could understand, accepting the romance between Coy Bryant and his wife while attending church with them and being friends.

There was no way Willie would ever have that discussion with Preacher Ed, and he decided by the time he got to the barn that he wasn't going to discuss anything with anybody anymore.

# CHAPTER 22

W ind and a light mist of rain was coming from the north. The clouds seemed to be moving out, but the cold wind and dampness were not helping Carl and Seth while they tried to dig a grave in the Rock Creek Cemetery.

Carl had discovered Willie's body lying across the poker table. When he stopped at Willie's and Ellen's on the way home, she told him Willie had gone to the barn after eating his dinner. He didn't understand why Willie would be at the barn this late. The sun was going down. Ellen told him Willie had eaten his dinner after Jim Rhodes visited him at the hog pen. He wasn't too concerned as he drove on to the barn. When he went in, he realized Willie was dead. Willie had been telling him for over a month that he was having trouble breathing after he ate. The doctor in Marshall told Willie it was probably heartburn, but his heart didn't sound good. Carl was shocked at the thought of Willie being dead. Without touching Willie, he picked up a note from the block of wood in the center of the room. Willie had died where he loved to spend his time.

The note was written with the chalk from the blacksmith shop said" Carl, I want you and Seth to dig my grave in the Rock Creek Cemetery. I hope you can do it without anybody else helping you.''

There was no signature, when he wrote the last letter of the "you", there was a scroll across the bottom, as if the last thing he tried to do was write something else.

Carl hadn't rushed back to the house to tell Ellen. He was still in the barn, waiting to try to decide what to do, when one of the Morrow boys stopped and came into the barn.

Carl looked at the grave they had started digging the day before. There was about a foot of water standing in the grave. He knew Willie wanted to be buried at Rock Creek, close to his grandpa Noah. Because the ground was so hard and rocky, it was like a tomb. You had to cut through the rock and the clay to dig a grave in the Rock Creek Cemetery.

Seth went to get a bucket to dip the water out, so they could start digging again. One of the Holliman boys suggested going to the Buffalo River and getting sand to put in the grave to dry up the water and to make the clay more manageable.

Seth got back with the bucket. They begin taking turns, getting down on their hands and knees and reaching into the grave and dipping out the water. The grave was about two and a half feet deep. When Willie had talked to Carl about being buried at Rock Creek, he had insisted that he didn't want one of the little shallow graves where people hit rock and didn't go deep enough.

"I want my grave five and a half feet deep, at least," Willie had said.

When Seth was dipping the water and Carl stood watching, Seth said "We are almost into the solid rock almost now, it's going to be tough going three more feet deep."

William Avey came back with a Holliman boy when they brought the sand from the river.

"Willie didn't want anybody digging the grave but you boys. Do you think you would care if we helped a little?" William asked.

Seth smiled before he answered, "We can forget Willie's rules; he's dead'.'

It was now a community effort to finish the grave. Seth and Carl had worked a long day after the day Willie died, and the digging had gotten tougher. They all begin to take turns digging and chiseling out the clay and rock. They got to the point that a huge boulder was uncovered in the center of the grave.

"We are going to have to use some dynamite," Carl said.

He had been at the cemetery digging other graves, and several times it became necessary to blast.

They began taking turns drilling holes for the powder. Seth had worked on the railroads and understood the blasting. "Drill one hole straight down, and drill the others at an angle, back toward the center of the rock,"

They followed his instructions. When the holes were finished, they loaded them with dynamite and attached enough fuses to allow them to get far away and out of danger of the blast.

The sound of the blast echoed through the hills. A crowd was gathering around the grave being dug.

Several stories begin to be exchanged about each person's relationship with Willie. At first, no one admitted to being a customer of his and buying moonshine, but as time went on, each person told a different story.

"Willie was the best man in the area," was the common description.

Carl spoke up. "I don't think any of his enemies have shown up here today."

He stepped out of the grave and shook hands with a

couple of his and Pauline's nephews. They were the children of Willie's oldest daughters; their fathers were still in the army and somewhere in Europe. It was rumored they would be coming home, and the war would be over by the middle of June. They were not old enough to go in the draft. They lived somewhere between Big Flat and the White River. Carl wondered how they heard about Willie and came to help.

The work went fast on the grave after everybody started cleaning up from the blast. Carl made sure the sides of the grave were straight and clean. They cleaned the pile of dirt far enough back for people to stand around the grave and have the funeral.

"Willie would be proud," he told Seth as they walked away from the grave.

It wouldn't be a sad day. The people who came to help with the grave were respectful. A common comment was, "We will miss him, and we will miss going to the bridge and getting moonshine or having him do our blacksmith work."

Carl went home. He wondered what Willie's funeral would be like. He could only imagine how hard it would be for Preacher Ed to conduct his friend's funeral.

# CHAPTER 23

There was no wind. The sun was shining, creating a warmth unusual for April. It was 1945. Carl went to the cemetery early and met Seth. Preacher Ed would bring Ellen Sitton, Willie's widow, to the funeral. Carl and Seth got there early to help the funeral home prepare the gravesite. They placed the tools for filling the grave in after the service away from the grave and leaning against the dirt. The funeral home brought an awning large enough to cover the area around the grave. They brought chairs and set them up on each side. They provided a podium for Preacher Ed to conduct the service.

When he met with Carl to plan the funeral, he said, "We can't take Willie inside the church building. I'll explain during the service at the graveside."

The cemetery was ready, and people were beginning to gather. The hearse would not arrive with Willie's body for two more hours. Carl and Seth planned on going back home and getting dressed for the funeral.

"We just as well stay in our overalls and work shoes,"

Seth said after the work around the gravesite was finished.

"I don't have a list of pallbearers that are supposed to carry the coffin from the hearse to the graveside," Carl answered Seth.

They spent the time while they were waiting for the funeral to start visiting with all the people who were arriving at the cemetery. It appeared most of the people in Big Flat were coming to the funeral. Cozy and Hickory Hollow residents were expected to be there. What surprised Carl was when a car with the sheriff's emblem on its side showed up. Sheriff Nick Reed had brought Joe Carson to the funeral. Two Davenport men from Yellville, a place in Marion County north of the Buffalo River, showed up for the funeral.

"Our grandfather spent two weeks with Willie setting up a sawmill, powered by a steam engine back during the railroad boom and construction," one of the men explained as he shook Carl's hand. "We have grown up listening to stories of Willie Sitton, the moonshiner."

Carl began to wonder how many people were going to be there. It was such a nice day, with bright sunshine and no wind. Plus, it was too early for the ticks and chiggers to be a problem.

*It is a perfect time of year to die*, thought Carl as he walked through the crowd, introducing himself.

He realized that to most people neither he nor Seth Tabor needed an introduction. While he didn't like being known as the witness to the murder or just as Willie Sitton's son-in-law, it was what most people recognized him for.

As he watched the hearse arrive, he wondered how many of the people were discussing different things about Willie Sitton. The Davenports came because of the cross ties being cut for the railroad. Some of the people came because of the stories about the moonshiner being best friends with the preacher. Others came because they had heard over the last year what happened when Coy Bryant and Sister Rhodes were shot.

Regardless of why they were there, it was time to carry the coffin to the graveside. Carl and Seth were on opposite sides as the coffin was rolled out of the hearse. Volunteer pallbearers took hold of the coffin, and they carried it and set it on the supports for lowering it into the grave. Preacher Ed needed to get there and start the service.

## CHAPTER 24

The crowd was seated underneath the canopy on both sides of the coffin. Pauline was seated next to her mother, with Carl sitting alongside her. Melissa Tabor and Seth were seated on the other side of Ellen Sitton. They were facing Pauline's sisters and their family sitting across from them on the other side of the coffin. Carl was very uncomfortable. Pauline was still whispering and complaining about him not coming back home and changing clothes before the funeral.

"I can't believe you're sitting here in your overalls and work shoes with mud on them and we're about to have my daddy's funeral." she said in a low whisper.

Carl believed he heard Melissa saying the same thing to Seth. They did not try to explain, but by the time they got the grave ready, people had been coming and they had run out of time to make it home and come back.

Preacher Ed arrived and started walking slowly toward the tent where Willie's body was sitting ready for burial. He would pause and visit people as he worked his way through the crowd. He still had not made it to the podium. Carl was becoming restless wondering just how long this was going to take. Just as he thought about going and asking Preacher Ed to hurry and start the service, he arrived at the podium.

Preacher Ed took hold of the podium with both hands. He stretched to make himself even taller as he took survey of the crowd. A hush came over the crowd as they suddenly became quiet.

"Lord, we're here today to pay our respects to Willie Sitton," Preacher Ed said.

He began the prayer, without changing the rhythm of his voice, he concluded by saying "And, we cannot add anything to his life. We do not need to explain anything about Willie Sitton. I came to Big Flat many years ago at the invitation of Jim Rhodes to preach a sermon. I've been here for many years. My wife, my children, and many friends are buried in the Big Flat cemetery. We're here today because of a very special person."

Preacher Ed stopped again and looked over the crowd as he had before he started speaking. He then spent several minutes telling the story of how he decided to convert the moonshiner. He told how that when a woman was beaten by her husband, and as he tried to counsel them, they usually blamed it on Willie Sitton's moonshine.

He talked about the decision he made about Willie's conversion. He talked about how surprised he was when he met Willie. He stood still with his face solemn, and some were close enough to see that his chin was trembling, and tears were welling up in his eyes.

"Should we wonder about Willie's conversion; I don't know if Willie needed converted. My greatest lessons in life were learned from Willie Sitton. I thought my troubles were the barrier that alcohol put between me and my ministry. I learned it's not what goes into our body that determines our righteousness. I made a terrible mistake one time when Willie and I shared our souls with each other. We also shared too much of his moonshine." Preacher Ed stopped. He took his handkerchief from his pocket and blew his nose. He folded it a different way and wiped his eyes. He reached inside his coat pocket and took out a little flask. He took a sip and replaced it in his pocket.

"I'm not going to explain any further about my relationship with Willie. I'm not going to talk about the times we spent sharing our opinions. Willie was the most disciplined person I ever met. He did the least harm to his fellow man of anyone I ever knew. He was the least jealous person I ever met. He was my friend. He taught me more than I ever expected to learn from anyone." Preacher Ed stopped and left the podium.

He first walked down the side of the coffin next to where Ellen, Carl, Pauline and the rest of the family, along with Seth and Melissa, were seated. He shook hands with each one of them, then he went to the other side where Willie's older daughters were seated and did the same thing.

He returned to the podium. After standing silently, he finally stretched his hands out as if to address the entire crowd.

"Who's going to miss Willie the most? It's going to be the people living at the Big Creek Bridge. It's going to be Ellen when she prepares a meal and his chair at the table is empty. It's going to be Carl and how he decides what work on the farm needs done next. It's going to be every one of you when you have that tool that needs to be sharpened. It's going to be this preacher when he comes up against a problem. I know for quite some time now, we will all be asking ourselves, 'What would Willie say?'" Preacher Ed bowed his head.

He didn't pray. It seemed like it was several minutes before he lifted his head and his hands and looked out at the crowd.

"It's time for us to go home. Willie's going home. We've got to leave his body here at the Rock Creek Cemetery. We will come back for years and share our stories about Willie Sitton."

Everybody stood up. Pauline was no longer fussing because Carl had not changed into clean clothes. There was no conversation among the people. They all began coming by and giving hugs to the family. No one knew what everyone was saying to each other. It was quiet and respectful as they all began to leave the cemetery.

Carl watched as the funeral director and his helper lowered the coffin into the grave. He waited before he stepped forward and said "Seth and I have to cover the grave ourselves. It's what Willie wanted us to do.

# CHAPTER 25

May was a cool month, but June was starting out hot.

Seth was cranking the bellows and the coals in the forge were beginning to turn red. He started firing the coal as soon as he made it to the shop and Carl was running late. While they were at the Rock Creek Cemetery for the decoration services, they decided they would finish sharpening all the tools in the blacksmith shop that Willie had not gotten around to doing before he died.

Carl doubted they could do it. Seth insisted they had both spent enough time in the shop working with Willie to get it done. They wanted to close out everything Willie had promised to do. When Carl arrived, he began laying out the tools to be sharpened according to the owners. There were several batches with seven or eight different owners.

"Why don't we sharpen garden tools first?" Seth suggested.

Carl didn't answer. He took the tongs and stuck a small hoe into the hot coals. Neither one of them was very conversational. Seth continued cranking the bellows and picked up the hammer as Carl took the hoe out of the forge.

"We're doing good on these hoes," Carl commented.

"Almost as good as Willie," Seth answered.

They spent the rest of the morning sharpening tools. When they decided to take a break for lunch, they were surprised to find Pauline had left their lunch sitting on the bench next to where they were working. They had not heard her when she left their lunch sitting almost in arm's reach of them.

They ate in silence. During the decoration, there was no discussion with either of them about Willie, Preacher Ed, or anyone else—or any questions about the shooting. They were both glad and hesitated to start a conversation as they worked.

"I'll miss Willie more than anyone," Carl finally commented.

"Yes, except for Ellen," Seth agreed with Carl.

"How much do you think you will miss him?

Seth didn't answer. He was thinking of the influence Willie had on both of their lives. He would never have met Melissa if he had not witnessed the rider leaving the barn. The friendship between Carl and Seth had grown since the trip to Alan Bryant's.

They went back to work and still were not in a mood to talk. Carl had spent most of the morning comparing what they were doing to the way Willie would have done it. The tools looked good. But were they tempered just, right? Would they last? All the questions remain unanswered.

It was a new era. Carl was now in charge of the farm. Willie left it to him and Pauline, and money was left to the older girls. Seth was not part of Willie's inheritance. Carl was planning on asking him to move into one of the farmhouses. He wanted to be close to his friend he had made because of them being the two witnesses to the murder.

Could it be made to work? Only time would tell. Until then every morning there would be a question. *What would Wiillie do?* His life would always cast a shadow over the people who knew him.

No one would ever know his thoughts about them. While he dealt with everyone in his way, he never criticized or gossiped about other people.

Willie and Preacher Ed continually evaluated the circumstances of the people they knew. But it was always a conversation they didn't share with anyone, except for Carl and Seth.

Their relationship was being continued by the friendship Carl Harris and Seth Tabor had developed. Willie's influence and Preacher Ed's guidance was what shaped their lives and friendship. Without realizing it, they continued in the same way. The discussion eventually came to the moonshine still.

"What are you going to do with Willie's still?'' Seth asked.

Carl didn't answer for several minutes.

"I don't think I'll make any moonshine. I know the formula for making Willie's moonshine," Carl commented.

Seth was amazed that Carl knew the recipe. He'd always heard how closely guarded the recipe was. He didn't ask when Carl learned the recipe, nor did Carl volunteer any information.

They spent the next few minutes discussing the moonshine business. They eventually talked about the discussions with their wives.

"Melissa told me she and Pauline had discussed it, and we were never going to make moonshine," Seth said.

Carl was not ready to admit that Pauline could tell him what to do. However, it appeared Seth was not going to go against Melissa's wishes.

"We don't need to make moonshine," Carl said. "That's something that Willie did, and I don't know how much money he made from it, but the farm is all the work I need. I will need you to help me do that more than fooling with the moonshine business"

The conversation ended while they were walking out into the center of the swinging bridge. Carl's mind went back to the beginning when he arrived at the bridge. The first sound he heard was Willie in the blacksmith shop. The echoing of the hammer hitting the anvil was forever fixed in his mind. After all these years he was standing in the middle of the bridge that he came across before he met Willie Sitton.

He had gone through a lot of changes but where he was standing was about the same as it was the day he arrived. Everything was normal and the creek was getting lower as the weather got hotter. The oak leaves and the other trees were drawing most of the moisture out of the hills. The water in the swimming hole was warm enough to swim. Seth and Carl continued to watch in silence as some young boys were diving off the rock where Willie always caught fish for his dinner. They listened to their laughter. Life was going on at the Big Creek Bridge. Willie Sitton's time had ended, and the moonshiner era along with it.

# Authors' notes

In summary of the moonshiner series, this is the last book about the lives of preacher Ed Tice and Willie Sitton.

I did my best to portray their lives, not as a struggle between two individuals, but as their efforts came together to find a common bond.

It is not a novel series meant to promote or condemn a lifestyle. I hope you don't see it as a moral conflict as each one of them lived according to their own values.

Let the Lord decide if preacher Ed failed also let him decide if Willie was too stubborn to become a real convert.

Don't look at any of this as an approval of a particular lifestyle or of drinking or any other thing portrayed in the novels. I have enjoyed writing this series of books. I hope you find time to read every one of them.

Thanks, Sam Pemberton

# ABOUT THE AUTHOR

Sam Pemberton was born on Bratton Creek, at an old homestead that hadn't changed much since the pioneer days. The year was 1944. Pemberton graduated from Big Flat high school. After their graduation in 1962, Sam married the love of his life, Patricia Treat.

He has worked construction in the drywall trade for most of his life. Sam presently lives in the beautiful Ozarks and continues in construction. He loves writing his stories and enjoys his morning coffee and porch time.

www.ingramcontent.com/pod-product-compliance
Lightning Source LLC
Chambersburg PA
CBHW070759120626
46557CB00002B/673